# Soul of the Matter

Michael A. Kroll

Published 2021
Print ISBN: 9798488070547
eBook ISBN: 978-1-68564-316-4
Cover photo by Michael A. Kroll
[www.michael-a-kroll.com](http://www.michael-a-kroll.com)[1]
Second Edition

---

1.     http://www.michael-a-kroll.com

Advance praise for
# *Soul of the Matter*
Available in print and audio

◈ "*Soul of the Matter* is the kind of book that grabs you in the first chapter and keeps calling to you until you get to the very last page. The story is beautifully told, but haunting. It talks about truths that none of us are comfortable with and it makes no apology. But Michael Kroll tells the story in a way that will keep you reading, and thinking, late into the night."

**Kevin Fisher-Paulson, *SF Chronicle* columnist and author,**

***A Song for Lost Angels* and *How We Keep Spinning...!***

◈ "This is storytelling at its finest. *Soul of the Matter* hooked me in the first five minutes when protagonist Harrison Ovitz witnesses a shocking act which takes him on an odyssey for answers that irrevocably change his life. Each character is richly developed, complex and memorable—people I grew to care about, and who have stayed with me long after I finished the last line. Michael A. Kroll is a master storyteller as well as a compelling narrator. In the audiobook version, his ability to convey trauma, humor, pathos, tension, forgiveness and compassion is masterful."

**Diane Reed, co-author, *Double Helix: A Memoir of Addiction,***

***Recovery, and Jazz in Two Voices***

◇ "*Soul of the Matter* is a very easy book to read. Rather than being a "Mystery Book," it is a book about a mystery and yet it does have many of the elements I like in a good mystery: food, odd characters, various geographical locations, and, most of all, an historical event about which I knew nothing."

**Joe Sternfeld, Actuarial, retired**

◇ "Damn! Just finished listening to *Soul of the Matter* here in my hammock. I'd listen to Michael Kroll's voice every day of the week if he did more! The storytelling is genius. I wish I was able to articulate what I meant by genius. He is an incredible storyteller, and I deeply appreciated all the exquisite layers."

**Galen Ellis, Community Health Planning Consultant**

◇ "Once I started listening, I couldn't stop... until the very last word. I wanted this story to end but dreaded that it eventually would. I loved this story..."

**Patricia Nelson, Seeker of Truth (and my longest friend)**

◇ "It has taken me a couple of days to sit with *Soul of the Matter* after listening to it. I may have to listen to it again because there was so much to it. I couldn't put it down... I was swept up by the imagery. It was so vivid... All the characters were well developed and I felt like I knew them."

**Jan Bourret, Manager, retired**

◇ "I found myself so connected to the main character and the story that I didn't want to stop listening. I kept inventing chores that needed to be done around the house so I didn't need to "put the book down." I loved the historical content and issues around race, policing, and bias. This was a great listen and I highly recommend it!"

**Ali Moss, Businesswoman**

# For the Fifty

# Preface

As a political writer on issues requiring fidelity to facts, to accuracy, and to real events, the idea of turning to fiction for the first time was intimidating. And yet, once begun, I found the story telling liberating, precisely because it freed me from those concrete restraints. At the same time, however, the seed that grew into *Soul of the Matter* was a very real event, and one which is described in the book with a journalist's precision. And, while the novel is not directly about this horrific event, it played such a role in the birth of the book, that it deserves a special mention here.

On July 17, 1944, just 35 miles east of San Francisco, a catastrophic explosion occurred at the Port Chicago munitions facility. 320 Navy personnel were killed on the spot, the vast majority of them African American sailors who had been ordered to do the dangerous mule work of loading waiting ships with bombs and other volatile munitions. The explosive force was so great, that nothing larger than the size of a suitcase remained of the 7,000-ton ship they had been loading. The shockwaves were felt as far away as Nevada.

When, after clearing the devastation – including the bits and pieces left of the dead and dying – the men were ordered to resume their work, hundreds chose, instead, to inaugurate a work stoppage to protest. Threatened with treason, a capital offense, all but 50 men decided to resume their dangerous work. The Navy charged those 50 – all Black – with mutiny; all were found guilty and sentenced to long years at the Federal Penitentiary at Leavenworth.

In our sad and shameful history with race, one can find no end of examples on which to focus, from slavery to lynching to voter suppression to stark inequities in criminal justice, in housing, in education, in health care, and in so much more. But for reasons known only to the muse, what happened at Port Chicago has haunted me ever since I first learned of it – and determined that Americans should not remain ignorant of this horror.

I first conceived of a conventional mystery format – a story of revenge by children of those court-martialed men visited on the children of those who had turned their fathers first into pack animals, and then into corpses or convicts. But soon, the story began to take on a life of its own. One by one, my characters came to life, leading me where they wanted the story to go. And where they wanted it to go was anything but conventional, turning a *Whodunit* into a *Whydunit*.

The result is the book you hold in your hand, *Soul of the Matter*.
Michael A. Kroll
August 4, 2021
Oakland, California

# Chapter One

It was after two in the a.m. and I was exhausted. As I swung easily into the arching two-lane on-ramp that merges into one before entering the San Francisco Bay Bridge in the far-left lane, I expected smooth sailing all the way home to Oakland. Thinking of the sleep that awaited me, I was beginning to drowse, dangerously, when I was suddenly aware that brake lights were coming on in front of me. Farther ahead, I could see the red glow of slowing cars. My old Datsun clattered to a stop, and I came fully awake, cursing out loud, in my manner.

"Unfriggingbelievable! Shid!"

A traffic jam! At this hour! Traffic wasn't just slowing, it had come to a complete stop. "Looks like a frigging parking lot," I sighed aloud, talking to the universe.

The stillness of the night was shattered by the cacophony of a hundred horns honking up and down the Bridge, as if the driver at the head of the pack had come to a halt merely to take in the view. I rolled the window back up and turned on my car radio, which I leave tuned to the all-night classical station, except when I want to be depressed. Then I listen to the news. The announcer was using his best mortuary voice to introduce Beethoven's 7th Symphony. I put the volume on high in the hopes of drowning out the growing din of automobile horns.

Ah, that first blast of symphonic horns, as much a testament to the creative genius of the human mind as the Bridge itself. Whatever was holding up traffic ahead, it looked like it was going to last awhile, so I tried to let the power of the music carry me to a different place. Instead, I found myself checking out my neighbors.

In my rearview mirror, I watched a kid with nose rings and straw-yellow hair tinged with alfalfa smoking a marijuana cigarette behind the wheel of his maroon BMW with a convertible top. He had flipped on the overhead light, recklessly unafraid of being seen.

Next to his rich-kids car, a brown and white Edy's Ice Cream truck was idling. If I'd had a cup of coffee in my hands, I could count all three of my favorite addictions assembled there.

A clearly furious Asian woman got out of her car ahead of me. It was one of those cookie-cutter designer cars that all look alike, and I couldn't tell if it was a Toyota or a Taurus, but it was pretty and red and sported a personalized license plate that said LACE.

She stood outside her door with her hand pressing on the horn through the open window, as if her angry impatience would jar loose the logjam. Once, she looked back in my direction as if for encouragement, but I gave none and she turned away, craning her neck to catch sight of whatever disaster lay ahead.

Abreast of me on my right was a beat-up old white pickup truck. On the dented door next to the driver, the words "JJ's Janitorial Service, Soul Proprietor" had been carefully painted in black. That "Soul Proprietor" caught my eye. Soul with a "u." Another example of the declining standards of literacy in the age of e-mail? I had to look up slightly to catch sight of the driver who was calmly speaking to someone on his cell phone, or rather, calmly listening to someone speaking to him on his cell phone.

The Asian woman's horn did not harmonize at all well with Beethoven, so I tried to tune her out. The kid behind me, still puffing away, was either singing or lip-synching to a rap to judge by the regular punctuation marks he made in the air with his head.

I turned my attention to Soul Proprietor next door. He looked to be in his mid-60s, but had one of those faces Black men sometimes have that make them look younger, even boyish, well into old age. As my eyes accustomed themselves to the dim light, I could see that he had a beautiful head of snow-white hair, and I mentally added ten years to the age I had given him.

There was something about this man that pulled me in. I never saw him utter more than one word at a time to his phone partner, nor did

I see any indication that anything was registering on that smooth face of his. He gave no token of what he was thinking or feeling if, indeed, he was thinking or feeling anything. And then, slowly, he glanced down toward me. Our eyes met just as the second movement of the magnificent 7th began its slow dirge.

I cannot describe the effect his eyes had on me. It was not merely the dark emotions conjured by the music that brought me to the brink of tears. It was him. It was those eyes that looked through me, beyond me to some distant place that only he could see. It was as if he, too, were listening to the grief-stricken lament of the music rather than to some disembodied voice on a car phone. There was such pain in his eyes, such sadness, and something else I could not quite identify. Anger? Fear?

"Fear." I said the word out loud and realized that it was I who was afraid. Afraid of what? Those eyes just kept looking at me without seeing, as if trying to understand what he was hearing. I smiled as warmly as I could, but his expression did not change, did not acknowledge my existence.

I shivered, and turned away. Fog was now pouring over the railing and onto the Bridge like special effects in some dream sequence in a Hollywood extravaganza. "Little cat's feet my arse," I heard myself say. It was more like a sudden, silent tide, cold as an anaconda.

The somber cellos kept beating out their dark, rhythmic tattoo as Beethoven's funereal strains moved towards their conclusion.

I shivered again, and turned back to Soul Proprietor. Still holding the phone, he was climbing out of his pickup and into the fog. Now he looked at me dead on, and his eyes seemed huge, as if he had taken LSD. But unlike the wild, vague stare of an acid head, JJ's eyes, his huge eyes, were now totally focused on mine. Our eyes were locked together, synchronized, and our heads swiveled in slow motion as he made his way between LACE, blaring her horn ahead of me, and my own car.

I reached up and locked the door. In return, he flashed me a menacing look that caused me to shiver again. He stopped and cocked his head slightly. A barely perceptible smile gave his face a quizzical look, as if to say, "Do you believe a simple lock can keep me from you?" I thought I saw him shake his head once, but it was too small a movement to be sure it wasn't just an involuntary tic.

And then he was walking again. Time seemed to slow down. I glanced in the mirror at the boy in the BMW behind me who was now watching us. Would he gallantly leap from his car and save me? Did I need saving?

I am not the kind of man who puts much stock in visions or ESP, or that sort of thing, but suddenly I had a premonition that death was near. Had I triggered something murderous in his demented head by locking my door? Was that mechanical act of self-protection his final indignity, one locked door too many?

My heart was pounding. Once more I turned my gaze on JJ – just in time to see Soul Proprietor put his right hand on the railing, his left still clutching his phone, look at me with such contempt I could not fathom its depth, and vault over the side of the Bridge.

# Chapter Two

The boy with the joint was out of his car before I could unlock and get out of mine. We reached the place where JJ had gone over at the same time, and peered down into the blackness.

"Did you see that? Awwwwwe-some!" He stretched the first syllable across two spans. "Fuck, did you see that?" he asked again. "Grampa musta been flying to do that shit." He was completely unaware of the irony of his choice of words. I noticed that he was very freckled, and I remember thinking, *Huh, he's a redhead under that yellow-green camouflage he wears for hair.* I focused on a clump of freckles under his right eye and said out loud, "Mmmm, that coffee smells good." Is that what it means to be in shock?

The Asian woman ahead of me, LACE, screamed twice, and then returned to laying on her car horn. I got the feeling her screams were more out of frustration at being stuck on the Bridge than in reaction to what had just happened. I'm not even sure she was aware of what had just happened.

And what had just happened? I couldn't be sure. A man was gone. A man who had crossed my path, who had been sitting not five feet from where I had been sitting, who had spoken to me through his sad eyes in a language I could not decipher, was gone.

Why? Why? What had I done to earn his last human expression of contempt? How could I make sense of any of it?

I stared down into the cold, dark abyss and wondered again at the mystery of the human mind, capable of creation that rivaled God's. And capable of destroying everything. The sound of far-off sirens grew more insistent as the crowd pressed around me, looking into the darkness. For what?

I can't tell you what I felt, not at that moment. I stood next to the car and tried to put out of my head what I had just seen. From the radio, I heard Beethoven's masterpiece racing toward its climax. Finally, like a zombie, I extricated myself from the crowd and made my way to the now-empty white pickup. Just inside the open driver's door, an ugly little brown dog with tufts of white fur sticking out here and there was asleep on the seat. I made a soft kissing sound with my lips, and he stood and stretched on short, spindly legs. He wasn't shy. He wagged his stubby tail, and I instinctively reached for him.

Don't ask what possessed me to take the dog. Other than shock and stupidity, I can't explain it. I felt something I could not identify. Was it a sense of responsibility? But how could I be responsible for the last choice Soul Proprietor would ever make? No, it wasn't responsibility, it was obligation. I owed JJ something. But what?

I carried the little dog to my car, cradling him against the damp fog, aware of the cold of his dog tag against my cheek. I opened my door and put him in, and he immediately found a comfortable spot on the front seat, turned twice, and lay down to sleep again.

Once more I made my way to Soul Proprietor's abandoned vehicle. JJ's Janitorial Service. Not any more, I thought, as I peered into the dark interior of the cab. A bowl of water on the floor had spilled slightly, and next to it I found a wet piece of paper, which tore when I put it in my shirt pocket. That was it. Whoever JJ was, he was very tidy.

The point at which he had sailed over the railing was now densely packed with people who had temporarily abandoned their cars. I looked up and around at the Bridge, this masterpiece of human creativity, and thought about Soul Proprietor far below, thought about him lying face down in the fog-shrouded waters, just another piece of flotsam amidst the telltale signs of humanity – paper and plastic, Coke cans and condoms – that washed beneath us on every tide.

I felt those melancholy eyes burning into mine, and I knew, knew I had to learn, had to try to understand at least who he was and why he was no more.

# Chapter Three

The sun was just breaking through the fog as I pulled into my driveway. It was after 8 in the morning.

The Bridge had been shut down by the kind of Cal Trans accident that commuters had come to expect, the kind that is invariably described as "freakish" and "unprecedented" by the state's highway construction bureaucrats. A huge, 100-ton concrete and steel overpass being put into place in the endless re-creation of California's freeways had somehow slipped its moorings, breaking free of its restraints and had crashed onto the roadbed 100 yards from the toll gates at the Bridge's east entrance, pulling down a giant crane attached to it. In fact, it was unprecedented. In its infinite wisdom, Cal Trans closed the onramps and exits in both directions, so nothing could move on or off the Bridge for more than five hours.

*At least Soul Man was spared this nightmare*, I thought, somewhat irrationally. And then, *Spare me those silver linings.*

As soon as I opened the door, JJ's little dog, which had been jumping back and forth between the front and the back seat for the last ten minutes of the ride, bounded over my lap, out the door, and made a beeline for the small patch of garden in my backyard, as if he had always lived there. You could almost see the expression of relief on his face as he relieved himself against the thick, pointed petals of the agave.

He did his business, then came running towards me, wagging that stub of a tail as if he belonged here with me. I picked him up and examined the worn dog tag he wore. On one side I read, My Name Is Pee-Pee.

Pee-Pee was on a line by itself. *Never was there a more appropriately named dog*, I thought. On the other side was an East Bay phone number that I assumed belonged to Soul Proprietor.

I put Pee-Pee down, and the two of us went inside. I scooped up the mail inside the door. It seemed like days since I had last slept, and

I was exhausted. Much too exhausted to sleep. I picked up the phone and dialed the number on the dog tag. I counted eleven rings before hanging up.

And then I remembered the amount of work that still had to be done to pull off the Charlene Benson-Black Benefit Dinner, our biggest fundraiser of the year.

Charlene was that beautiful little six-year-old child in New York the media discovered too late. For years, her father had pinched and slapped and jerked her by the arms, and shaken her until her bones broke while school counselors and teachers, like her mother, maintained an innocent silence. And they all might have remained silent forever except that one rainy afternoon, Daddy beat his daughter to death. One of thousands.

Charlene's death led directly to F.A.C.T. — Fostering Abused Children Together — which, fourteen years into its existence, hired me as its principal fund raiser. Actually, F.A.C.T. lured me away from the National Coalition for Equal Justice the old-fashioned way, by paying me more than twice as much to do the same work. The NCEJ is a good cause, but so is F.A.C.T., and one good cause deserves another.

Despite being one of the hokier acronyms I had worked for, I had already raised nearly five and a half million dollars for F.A.C.T. over the past three years, counting grant money, individual donations, and the Annual Dinner. I was good at what I did. It came naturally to me, an irony not lost on those who knew how difficult I found it to earn a decent living on my own behalf.

Until now, that is. F.A.C.T. paid more than a fair salary for my efforts — a rare change from what I had come to expect from the dozens of non-profits I had raised money for over the past fifteen years. That was the main reason I hadn't followed my usual pattern and walked away after a year or two searching for something new, something more stimulating, something more to do with the operating of the machinery and not just the drilling for the money that kept it greased. I had more than once thought of ditching F.A.C.T. for good, but I was earning too much. I had even managed to save a little. My nest egg would fit a hummingbird's nest, but saving anything was a novel experience. And money is a strange thing. It both liberates and imprisons.

The "Big Dinner" was just weeks away, and I was beginning to enter the panic mode that had characterized my two previous, and very successful dinners. Had I thought of all the high rollers who should be approached for the $1,000-a-plate tickets? Who should print the invitations after the botched job the Offset Printing Center did last year? How many more twenty-hour days could I put in? The fact that it was 1999, making this the last "Big Dinner" of the 20th Century, added an entire new layer of stress.

The truth is I was getting tired. Sure, the long hours contributed to that feeling. It's a lot easier to stay up all night when you're twenty-something with all your hair than when you're a prematurely balding, middle-aged man past fifty. But there was something else. I was beginning to hate fundraising. Even for a cause I believed in, and I believed in F.A.C.T.

I couldn't sleep, but I could eat. I brewed a fresh pot of coffee and went to the freezer. I settled on a pint of Key Lime Prime and Passion Fruit Fantasy ice cream, something light. I saved the more substantial flavors, like Chewy Chocolate Chunks, for dinner. In the back where I always keep it, I found the only container of vanilla in the freezer and took it out, too.

I spooned out a bowl full of the green stuff that passed for key lime and put it on the floor for Pee-Pee who licked it a couple of times, opened and closed his funny little mouth, and walked away. "Don't expect dessert," I said to Pee-Pee's retreating behind. I picked up the envelope on top of the stack of mail and scribbled Dog Food on it as a reminder. And then, as an afterthought, in block letters I wrote in a firm hand: RETURN TO?

The smell of fresh brewing coffee filled my small kitchen. I opened the gallon container of vanilla and carefully lifted out the shallower quart of still untouched ice cream that I used as a false bottom. From the now ice cream-free carton, I fished out my marijuana stash and the little wooden pipe I keep hidden there. I broke off a small, red, sticky bud from a larger clump, tore it into crumbs, and filled the pipe. I took a deep, long puff and let the smoke fill my lungs as the drug filled my head. Ahhhhhhh. Shards of memory competed for my attention — the straw-haired boy, the fallen freeway, the memorial dinner. JJ did not surface.

Between puffs, I spooned the colorful ice cream directly from the containers to my mouth, savoring the cold, creamy concoctions. I shuffled through the mail until I came to a letter addressed to Harry S. Truman Shakovitz. A letter from my mother. I hadn't been Harry S. Truman Shakovitz since high school graduation when I gave myself the gift of a new name. But she had named me Harry S. Truman, and that is what she insisted on calling me, whether I liked or not. I did not.

Anyway, I opened my mother's letter and tried to read, though my extreme exhaustion and the marijuana made it hard to concentrate.

"Dear Harry," I read about six times. "Have you read about what they are doing to the ozone? I really think you might want to consider raising some money in that effort."

She meant, of course, in the effort to stop what they were doing to the ozone. My mother's passion for the political point always polluted her prose. Anyway, she knew I would know what she meant.

I was born on November 2, 1948, in Chicago. The headline in that evening's Tribune made no mention of this momentous event. Instead, it announced "Dewey Defeats Truman!" My very political mother, a dedicated New Dealer who had walked precincts for Give 'Em Hell Harry (whom she called Give 'Em Heck Harry), decided right then and there to name her newborn little yuck after the just-elected president. Yuck. Yuck.

My mother, Gladys Shakovits – nee Gladys Shakovits – was a strange combination of political radical and personal prude. She never tolerated cursing of any kind in our house, for example. The only time I tested that policy, I got my mouth washed out with soap. I was nine years old. My fourth-grade friends, Vincent and Henry, had just discovered the "F" word and we had been trying it out all afternoon. We giggled each time one of us said it until it seemed like nothing more than a joke. When I went inside, I still had a big smile on my face. "Mama," I asked in mock innocence, "is fuck one of the words you won't let me say?"

Without a word, she grabbed me with her right hand clamped to the scruff of my neck, her left propelling me forward straight into the bathroom. In one fluid movement, she turned on the tap, picked up the bar of hand soap and let the running water make a foamy suds in her cupped left hand. Then she shoved my head down into the sink, and rubbed her soapy hand into my mouth. Hot tears streamed down my face purely out of humiliation. It was the last time I ever uttered a curse word without adulterating it into something slightly different. Which, in high school — along with my name — made me something slightly different.

All the way through Valley Elementary School and Reznik Unified High School (which quickly was dubbed, R.U. High), my delightful classmates had morphed my name from Harry S. Truman Shakovitz to Harry Ass Shakovitz. Everyone called me Harry Ass, including more than one gym teacher along the way. I vowed that as soon as I had the power, I would change my name. Somehow, high school graduation seemed to confer that power on me. I decided to move out of the Shak and call myself Ovitz, a last name, which required something more formal than Harry to introduce it. I became Harrison Ovitz. Freedom comes in many forms.

Besides my mother and sister, and the occasional geek from school days I ran into in my fundraising efforts, nobody but the mailman —

a woman, actually, a Vietnamese immigrant — knew my real name. I had to explain it to her when she balked at delivering my mother's carefully addressed letters. She laughed about it for a long time. In fact, for a while she took to greeting me with a smile and a jaunty, "Good morning, Mr. Ass," whenever she caught me at home. I wiped the smirk off her face, though, when I threatened to withhold the traditional box of See's candy I gave her at Christmas.

My mother had actually grown more radical over the years, though her political focus had changed countless times right along with the times. She was not against putting her body where her mouth was, either. She had gone to jail eleven times at my last count. She had marched on the Pentagon to protest nuclear testing in the '50s, given money to the Panthers in the '60s, decried the Israeli treatment of the Palestinians in the '70s, stood in front of a train carrying ammunition bound for Central America in the '80s. She had even managed to get to ground zero during an A-bomb test in Nevada, earning her the dubious title of Atom Mama by her jailers there.

Lately, though, her single concern had been for what she called our "Mother Mudball" — the earth itself. Today it was ozone. Yesterday, the rainforest. Tomorrow, the ocean. I have no doubt that had I been born in 1998 instead of 1948 she would have named me Savemothermudball Shakovitz.

My father? Well, he's another story. One that I don't feel like telling. Suffice it to say that one of the reasons I had not walked away from my fundraising responsibilities at F.A.C.T. was that I had plenty of personal experience in the American pastime of child abuse. What I suffered at my father's hands, and any other weapon he could get hold of, permanently crippled my ability to trust adults, pretty well dooming the few tentative efforts I have made at loving relationships. Children don't need to be protected from pornography, they need to be protected from the adults in their lives. The only thing I care to say about my father is that the day after he walked out on my sister and mother and me, my mother dropped his last name and we all reverted to her birth name. I just wish it hadn't been Shakovitz.

# Chapter Four

My mother's predictable but strangely comforting letter — I really *was* tired — was the most interesting piece of mail in the pile, mostly a collection of "Fantastic Offer" money-to-borrow schemes at practically no interest, "New Platinum Plus" credit card offers where they practically GIVE you the money, and "Save the Union" solicitations to donate just a pittance to the Democratic Party. Not to mention the bills that tended to overwhelm my thinking whenever I toyed with the idea of leaving my job — as I had done so many times before without regret.

The *Chronicle* was stuffed into the mail slot where my paperboy — who, of course, is an elderly, stooped Laotian woman — had been stuffing it ever since my neighbor complained about it landing in her driveway. I scanned the front page and the inside jump pages, then remembered that the paper would have already been put to bed by the time JJ took his flying leap. It seemed so long ago, but it had only been a few hours.

I took my ice cream breakfast into my office, which doubles as the bedroom, stepping over little mounds of papers, like the piles of dirt gophers leave next to their holes. Each paper pile represents a different fundraising project — and take my word for it, although I practice the art of Chaos Management, it never takes me long to find what I'm looking for.

I sat on the edge of the still-made bed and switched on the TV. Like an elastic attachment, Pee-Pee was in the room, on the bed and in my lap all in one movement. I picked him up with one hand and deposited him on the bed next to me. He looked at me sadly, like I had betrayed him too, somehow. "Fug you, Dog," I said out loud, turning back to the television.

From the corner of my eye I watched him chase his ratty little tail around three times before he lay down. With an audible doggy sigh, he closed his eyes and went to sleep. Almost immediately, his right leg began to twitch. *Post-Traumatic Stress*, I thought. The tortured dreams of seeing his master abandon him, abandon the world itself.

The Headline News provided the usual breakfast, lunch, dinner and in-between-snack fare: an arson fire in Oakland resulting in the death of a nine-year-old Vietnamese girl; a munitions explosion at a U.S. military base in Hawaii, three men killed; an arsenal discovered in a high school gym locker in Dekalb, Illinois after a teacher is shot; student scores dropping everywhere; and Congress debating whether to make burning the flag a capital offense.

And then, suddenly, there it was. A Black commentator stood on the San Francisco side of the Bay with the Bay Bridge beautifully etched behind him, reflecting silver light in the morning sunrise. "Early this morning, two unprecedented events became permanent parts of the history of the San Francisco-Oakland Bay Bridge that you see rising up behind me," he said, looking earnestly into the lens of the TV camera and smiling incongruously. "First, a giant steel girder came crashing down at three-twenty-three this morning, shutting off all access to or exit from the Bridge just a 100 yards from the East Gate Toll Booths. And while many are calling it a miracle that nobody was killed in that freak accident, the same claim cannot be made about the Bridge itself. While all Bridge traffic came to a standstill, according to an eyewitness, a man got out of his pickup truck just west of Treasure Island there behind me, walked calmly to the railing, and threw himself into the frigid waters of the Bay below."

There was more about the falling girder, but I paid no attention. So it was real. It had really happened. I hadn't been hallucinating. TV confirmed what I doubted of my own experience. And suddenly, there she was, LACE, their eyewitness, looking ravishing, as if she thrived on suicide and sleeplessness.

"It was just terrible," she gushed. "I've never seen anything like it. He just jumped off the edge, and we were stuck there for the next five hours. It was just... terrible!"

The announcer was intoning something about the victim's identity being withheld pending notification of next of kin, but I wasn't paying any attention. I sure wasn't going to learn the "why" from people who couldn't even tell me who.

But the words "next of kin" stirred something. I thought of Soul Man's poor next of kin, as Pee-Pee stirred next to me. "I'll find someone to take you," I promised.

The question was how. Theoretically, I was supposed to be back at the office in an hour, but that would have been impossible even if I could have turned my world right-side up again. I just can't live on an hour or two of sleep a night. And wishing I could make my world normal again was like wishing the Indians had won the wars with the U.S. government — it's enough to bring a smile to your face, but it doesn't get you very far.

Suddenly, I remembered that JJ had been thoughtful enough to leave a note. As delicately as I could, I fished the torn paper from my shirt pocket and laid it on the nightstand next to the headboard. It hadn't dried completely and it tore some more as I tried to smooth it, but JJ had had a clear, firm hand so even the damage the water had done couldn't entirely smudge out the printed message: K A U F M A N B L DG/ 661-9328.

I picked up the phone and dialed. "You need to dial an area code," came the pre-recorded message. "*Of course,*" came the immediate thought. "*It's a 415 number. He was coming from work!*" I dialed again.

Pee-Pee stood and stretched, and wagged his hairless tail. I patted his head, which he took as an invitation back into my lap. I was about to uninvite him when a man answered, "Kaufman Building, Main Lobby, James speaking, how can I help you?"

"You can help me by connecting me to Personnel, James," I said. "This is Channel 3 calling." Fundraising had taught me that people never get over the thrill of being on TV or even being near it. Offer the suggestion that TV might be in their future, and people are willing to open doors for you. If I was uncomfortable cursing, lying came naturally to me.

"Sure thing," James replied in his most attentive voice. "You got it." And sure enough, I got it.

"Excuse me," I continued to the woman with the breathy voice that now greeted me, "could you tell me if you have a janitor with the initials JJ?"

"I beg your pardon."

"I'm looking for a janitor, initials JJ," I said. "What don't you understand?"

"Sir, we are not a janitorial service. I suggest you consult the yellow pages if you're looking for a janitor." *Oh yeah*, I thought. *Look down your contemptuous nose at me, lady. You can't even understand what the hull I'm asking you!*

"No, lady," I spat, "I'm not interested in finding a janitor. I'm interested in your janitor. His name is JJ and I'm his son and a lawyer. If you can't tell me about my father's employment, perhaps a lawsuit would pry it out of you. Can you spell your name for me?"

"If you are talking about Mr. Jeppards," she spat back, "I can tell you that we had to let Joshua go last night after he finished his shift is what I can tell you!" She hadn't meant to. A name! JJ — Joshua Jeppards. It had just come out in a fit of anger at my overbearing rudeness. I could tell she was surprised that the words had come out of her mouth. But surprise didn't begin to convey the stew of emotions I was feeling — shock, understanding, grief, and even a dash of the relief that comes with knowledge.

"What about family," I asked, aware of my mistake the minute I uttered it.

"I thought you said you were his son," she tried to thunder in her breathy voice. I wanted to laugh. I needed to sleep.

"Not his blood son," I said, "but just like..." She hung up in mid-sentence. Too late, though. She had already solved the mystery. JJ jumped because they sacked him. Maybe he had been with them for years. Maybe he was close to retirement. Maybe he was tired. Whatever, they fired him, and he did himself in. So that was that.

I lay back on the bed and pictured for the hundredth time that somber and dignified man staring into my eyes before closing his forever. I closed my eyes. Pee-Pee adjusted himself onto my belly. Unconsciously, I rested one hand across his scrawny back, as I drifted towards a restless sleep, briefly jerking awake as I pictured Pee-Pee jumping from a ledge and hurling down towards the dark waters of my dreams.

Before sleep overtook me, I thought incongruously about all the jobs I had had since my first, as a teenager cleaning the hot grease from the grill in a pre-MacDonald's hamburger joint, "Five For a Dollar" (if you also bought five large, slightly soggy fries and sodas). Even if I included my current job with F.A.C.T., there wasn't one I'd rate worth a cat's arse, much less my own.

# Chapter Five

I awoke with a start, immediately anxious, like I was forgetting something. A dream? No, I had slept hard for an hour. No dreams disturbed that sleep of the dead. Something about the dead?

As sleep cleared from my mind, I was aware that Pee-Pee was on the bedstand licking up the melted ice cream that had flowed across page 11 of the B section of the *Chronicle*. "I gotta get you some real food, I guess," I said, as if by saying it I would assure its getting done. As I picked Pee-Pee up, my eyes fell on an article that I myself had placed. "Annual Dinner a F.A.C.T. of Life" the clever headline editor had attached to my article, which, like the others, I did not read.

The Dinner! I had forgotten about The Dinner. The incredible number of things yet to do. My job.

The phone rang just twice at the office before Audrey's voice announced that I had reached Fostering Abused Children Together and asked if she could help me.

"A couple hundred thousand bucks would help me immeasurably," I said, deadpan, without further identifying myself.

"Yeah," she laughed, "who wouldn't it help? Where are you, Harry?"

Audrey was the only person besides my mother I permitted to call me Harry. She had done it from the moment the boss, Dorothy Lehrman, had introduced us. "Audrey Vance," she had said, "I want you to meet our new fundraiser, Harrison Ovitz." To which Audrey had said, "Welcome aboard, Harry" with such genuine warmth and sincerity that I couldn't bear to correct her. And though she had since heard me make that correction many times – "Actually, it's Harrison, if you don't mind" – she correctly concluded it didn't apply to her.

I had never arrived at the office later than 8 in the morning, so her question was genuine. "I'm at home, Audrey," I said. "I worked late last night."

There was silence at the other end as Audrey waited for the real explanation. When it didn't come, she prompted. "So?"

"Did you hear about the mess on the Bridge early this morning? Well, I was in it."

"What mess, Harry?" Audrey rode her bicycle the three miles from her apartment. To her, rush hour meant an extra five minutes as she expertly threaded her way through traffic.

"Take my word," I said. "I need to talk to Dorothy."

"Dottie's in a meeting," she said sweetly. No one but Audrey dared to call Dorothy Dottie. "Shouldn't you be at the same meeting?" she added.

"Tell her something happened. Tell her I'll be in later. Tell her..."

"What's wrong, Harry?" Audrey demanded, cutting me off. "Something's wrong, I know it is. I know you, Harry, and something has to be wrong. I'm going to get Dottie."

Pee-Pee scratched to get out at the same moment I heard Dorothy click into the line to ask, "What's this all about, Harrison?"

I gave her the two-bit version of what had happened to me since leaving the office.

"I heard about that guy jumping off the Bridge when I was coming into work this morning," she said. "Wow."

"Heard about it? From whom?" I asked.

"The radio, Shid Head," she laughed. "Haven't you heard of the radio?" Good. She called me Shid Head which she had done since hearing my first curse, but only when she was feeling playful, which wasn't often.

"The radio," I echoed. My mind was in that thick zone brought on by lack of sleep and grass. I had forgotten about the radio.

"I've got to go, Dorothy."

"When are you coming in?" Uh-oh. It was that "you're-an-employee" voice she used when she thought she had to exert control. "When are you coming in?" More insistent.

Once again, my mind started to swirl like the waters into which Soul Man had plunged. "It's not a good time," I heard Dorothy say. "Harrison. I need you this afternoon. The Dinner. We're meeting with the Board about the Dinner. Harrison?"

"I'll call you back." I said.

*Winter*, from Vivaldi's *Four Seasons*, was about to end as the radio came to life. It took me a minute to switch to the all-news station. I listened to some of the same stories whose headlines I had read before falling asleep – the base bombing, the school shooting. I let Pee-Pee out the back door. I poured myself a cup of tepid coffee and was about to heat it in the microwave when I heard it. A man had jumped over a railing of the Bay Bridge shortly after three this morning bringing traffic to a standstill. (*They got their chronology reversed*, I thought, *but the basic facts were there.*)

The man's identity was being held pending notification of next-of-kin. A witness had reported a motorist taking something from the dead man's truck, and police were now searching for him.

LACE! I sank down into the sofa. She had seen me go to Soul Man's pick up, seen me nestling Pee-Pee against my chest as I returned to my car. She had called the cops and they were looking for me. Dorothy wanted me at the office. The cops... they just wanted me.

# Chapter Six

I knew what I had to do, but I hated the thought of doing it. It's not that I wanted to get back to work, but if I didn't do what was required to make the Annual Dinner pay off, I wouldn't have a job for long. I sure didn't want cops to come sniffing around the office, asking a bunch of questions that I'm not even sure I could answer. So I checked the number on the card I kept in my wallet, made the dreaded phone call, and got the switchboard.

"Oakland Police Department, Officer Korvin speaking. How can I direct your call?" I could have identified myself to Officer Korvin and let him decide where to direct me, but instead, I asked for Perry. "Officer Ely, please." I was immediately put on hold and subjected to elevator music, the kind that pretended to be high-brow, but hardly ever got higher than an edited version of the Nutcracker Suite. Korvin came back on the line. "Ely's at lunch. He just left. Would you care to speak with another officer, or can I give you his voice mail?"

*They'd had their be-polite-to-the-public speech this morning*, I thought, and hung up without answering him. I knew where Perry took his lunch because I'd eaten there with him on more than one occasion. We had met three years before at the YMCA. He did the whole workout routine, and his body showed it. When he worked up a sweat that dripped off his biceps, it glistened off his shoulders, the color of light caramel, a delicious mixture of black and brown, with a hint of Polynesian gold. I, on the other hand, had joined only to swim laps, and never worked up a sweat at all. If I had, nobody would have noticed.

We liked each other from the beginning, and our small talk, as we stood in front of our lockers at 5:30 in the morning, slowly gave way to more pointed comments about various of our fellow gym jocks. "That guy should give up his comb-over and just glue it in place," Perry would say, giving his head the slightest nod in the direction of the balding man desperately combing the five strands of hair he still had hanging off one side.

"Hey, hey, take a look at that arse walking away," I'd say, just loud enough for Perry to hear. "Wasn't he the model for the Pillsbury Dough Boy?"

Perry Ely was an impressive looking man. The routine he completed every morning at the Y was only a part of a lifelong regimen of good diet, good exercise, and none of the kind of bad habits that put on the pounds that the gym crowd paid big bucks to take off. He was strikingly handsome, though compact and rather short. The ten-thousand-watt smile he flashed was as genuine as the police switchboard operator's bright civility had been fake. Lilla, his wife of seven years, had told me over dinner once that it was that smile that had hooked her from the beginning. Being Lilla, she added as if in afterthought, that smiles were rare from her vantage point as lead attorney in the Public Defender's Criminal Division, so Perry had a low bar to get over.

Although she didn't say it, I noted that whenever we went out together that she didn't much appreciate the constant attention his good looks and brilliant smile attracted from women, young and old. (At those times, Perry made a show of pretending not to notice the furtive glances, the up-and-down appraisals of the whole package, the returning smiles, to which Lilla would sneer, "You're not fooling anyone.") Even some men – even I – would sometimes give him the appreciative once-over. He was that attractive.

In truth, I admired Perry's good looks, but there was much more than just his appearance to recommend him. He shattered all my preconceptions about what it meant to be a cop. For one thing, we shared a love of classical music, and in particular, Beethoven. But music was only the tip of Perry's iceberg. It went deep, and you had to get to know him before its contours began to truly reveal themselves. He was a voracious reader, and not just the classics, but offbeat philosophers and writers of all kinds, forcing me to read what he was reading so that I could keep up with him. He had scored very high on the law school entrance exam, and had even paid his deposit to Stanford Law School, when a little voice went off in his head saying, "*Why are you doing this? You don't want to be a lawyer.*" And, over his mother's loud objections (she did want him to be a lawyer), he joined the police force, which he had wanted to do since he was six.

The only drawback to Perry's personality – the one thing that kept him from moving up the ranks into management – was his utter unwillingness to suffer fools gladly. His toasts at police functions were famous for calling a spade a spade, for lampooning the latest management reorganization efforts, and – significantly – for denouncing the racism and sexism that his fellow officers routinely displayed in their professional and personal lives.

We became the kind of friends who invited each other over for meals, the kind who go out together for a movie and a beer. Plus, I had come to rely on him both for my ongoing fundraising efforts – he knew everybody in local government – and, more particularly, for his own considerable efforts to make the Charlene Benson-Black Benefit Dinner the great success it had become. Perry had his own history with child abuse, not as a victim, but as a police investigator who had seen things he wished he could wipe out of his mind. He told me that it took all his efforts, whenever he came into a situation where a child had been hurt by a parent, not to return the favor right there on the spot. On those days, he'd go home after work and take 4-year-old Sasha and 7-year-old Ayusha in his arms and hold them, until they wiggled free.

It was time to pay Perry a visit.

I let Pee-Pee out, and he went straight to the garden and came running back, like he'd lived there all his life. "Come on, you little worm," I said. "We're going for a ride."

I left him sleeping comfortably on the front seat as I went into Casa de Mama, the Mexican restaurant across the street from the jail, where

I knew I'd find my friend. He was sitting where he always sat, at the corner flirting with Eva, the Cuban waitress, a routine the two of them had practiced so often that it played like a well-rehearsed TV sketch.

"So, when are we going to consummate this relationship," Perry teased.

"You call this a relationship?" She bantered. "My cat's better company than you."

"I don't want to be catty, but when are you and El Gato planning to tie the knot?"

I'd heard it all before, so didn't hesitate to interrupt.

"Perry!" I spoke more sharply than I had intended. *Modulate*, I thought to myself. Exhaustion was taking its toll. "Perry," I continued, somewhat less aggressively, "I need to talk to you."

Still chuckling at his own little joke, Perry turned to me and smiled. "Harrison," he said warmly, as if inviting me to join them in a verbal threesome. "Harrison, my friend, what can I do for you?"

"We have to talk."

"Okay, talk," he said, unaware that the mood was about to turn dark.

"Sorry, Perry, but this is actually about police business. I have to talk to you alone."

# Chapter Seven

Perry looked at me strangely. He winked at Eva, slid a fiver across the counter toward her, and walked over to the cashier to pay for his lunch. I followed him out and across the street to the police station where he led me to a cramped room in the basement with a table in the middle. He took a seat on one side, motioning me to sit opposite him. Neither of us said a word.

From his side of the badly scarred table, he waited a minute before prompting me. "Okay," Perry deadpanned, breaking the silence. "You now have my undivided attention. You've already ruined my lunch, so what's so important that you had to see me alone?"

"It's me," I said. It sounded stupid even as I said it, but I didn't know where to start. "I'm the one you're looking for."

"What the hell are you talking about?"

"Sorry, Perry." I started again. "I'm tired. I'm really tired. I haven't had much sleep since..." My voice broke. It took me a second to gain control and continue. "...Since he went over the side."

Perry looked at me as if this was the beginning of an elaborate practical joke. He smiled broadly, but then looked serious again, trying to decide whether I was serious or not. He waited for more, but I needed more prompting. Ask me something, I wanted to scream. "I'm serious," I said, as if that explained everything.

"About what? Serious about what?"

I took a deep breath, and launched. "That guy. That guy who went over the Bay Bridge this morning. The radio said you're looking for me."

Suddenly, I was there. My hands were sweaty, and I could hear my heart beating fast in my ears. I wasn't aware that my breathing was keeping pace with my racing heart, until Perry snapped me back to the present.

"Take a breath, Harrison." This was the professional cop taking command of the situation. The smile was gone. This was Officer Ely in full police mode. It wasn't a request; it was an order. "Calm down and tell me what you mean." Suddenly, my fear ebbed as it had come, like the passing of a shudder. His tone was softer, more familiar. "Are you talking about the janitor? The janitor that stopped all the traffic last night?"

"How did you know he was a janitor," I replied, like I was in a novel, like I was the detective interrogating him.

"The truck. He thoughtfully left his truck on the Bridge before he left the Bridge himself."

"Don't joke!" This time it was me issuing a command. The volume of this command surprised both of us.

Perry looked at me in a new way. For the first time, I saw the same sympathy that I saw in his eyes whenever he spoke of a crime against a child. Except now it was me he felt sympathy for. As if I were a child. Strangely, it calmed me, cleared the fog.

"The truck," Perry said, gently. "We were talking about the truck."

"Oh, yeah. 'JJ's Janitorial Service'," I remembered. "Jeppards," I said. "Joshua Jeppards."

"How do you know his name?" Perry asked, his voice hardening. "As far as I know, that information hasn't been released. If so, it sure hasn't been given to the public. I'm not even sure they have an ID yet."

A clear-headed objectivity seemed to wash over me, a state of mind which I believed allowed me to function at all. It was as if I were seeing the whole thing from a height. I could look down and describe what I saw without fear, even if I was part of the scene I was describing.

"Traffic was already stopped," I corrected Perry's description, as if that were the most important detail of the story. "Traffic was already stopped." A random thought popped into my head, and I made a mental note to observe where we choose to start the stories we tell. And then I remembered where I was and what was going on.

"He was talking to someone on the phone and then he just threw himself over the edge. He just, I don't know... He just looked at me and then he went over the side!"

"You were there? Were you with him?"

And there it was again! The tightening in my stomach. "Yes," I wanted to scream. "I was with him. I am with him now. He drew me in with his murderous eyes. He drew me in and then disappeared, as if that ended it... He stared right through me before he... before..." Soul Man was there again, his eyes locked on mine as he made his deliberate way to the ledge. I felt the cold fog and shivered involuntarily.

Perry got up and filled a paper cup with cold water from an old-fashioned water cooler in the corner. He put it in front of me, and I took a sip. What passed for calm returned much more quickly this time.

"I'm the one you're looking for."

Perry waited a beat before asking, "Looking for?"

"The radio said you have a witness that saw someone take something from his truck and you're looking for him. I mean me. You're looking for me."

"You?" You could almost see that proverbial light go off in his head. "Did you take something from his truck?"

"A note. I took a note. That's how I know where he worked."

"That all," Officer Ely pressed, the policeman taking over.

"Oh yeah. And a dog."

"What did you do with 'em?"

I looked up over his shoulder out the tiny high window to see if I could see my parked car, but all I could see was a part of the gate where cops drove criminal suspects into the guts of the building to hurry their usually-young charges through intake and into the jail above.

"The note's at home. The dog's outside in the car."

Perry stared, waiting for me to continue.

"I know why he did it, Perry."

"What do you mean you know why he did it? Did he talk to you?"

"No, but his employer did. I passed myself off as his son, and they told me they had to fire him last night. He was on his way home from work, just like I was, only he didn't have a job to go back to. That was it."

At first, Perry just looked at me across the table. Then he started to laugh. "Black janitor fired, kills self," he laughed, spreading his hand in the air across an imaginary banner headline. He shook his head in disbelief.

"Why is that so funny, Perry? I don't get it."

"That's because you've never been Black," he said, now all serious. "Black people don't kill themselves when they lose their jobs. If they did, there'd be a whole lot more Black people taking themselves out."

"But I saw him. He jumped, Perry. He knew what he was doing."

"Oh, I'm not saying he didn't commit suicide. I'm saying that losing his job isn't why he did it. I'd think a man in your business would know that Blacks have the lowest rate of suicide. White men kill themselves when they lose their jobs, not Black men. Even Asians have a higher rate of suicide than we do. No, Harrison, something else had to be going on for this guy... What did you say his name was?"

"Joshua Jeppards."

"Yeah. Old Joshua got some news he couldn't handle. Maybe he got an HIV diagnosis. Didn't you say he was on the phone before he did it? Maybe it was his doctor giving him the bad news. Cancer. Or maybe his wife just died and he can't go on without her. Whatever it was, it had to be bigger than just losing his job. Even Blacks on death row don't do the state's work by taking themselves out. White guys do. They can't handle the pressure. Never had to. But us? Goddammit, man, Blacks have lived with that pressure since arriving here in chains! They don't kill themselves over it. They fight. We fight! And we endure."

His voice had grown loud, and the pitch had risen during this little lecture. There was an edge in his voice that I had heard before whenever the subject turned seriously to issues of race. "There are things you just don't get," the edge in the voice seemed to say. I always heard in that rawness a kind of unspoken warning, as if to say, "You can't understand what it means to be Black, so don't pretend you can."

There was silence between us for a minute. Then Perry stood and walked around the table to where I sat. He put a comforting arm around my shoulder. "Harrison, you have to give a statement. Not to me, though. This isn't an Oakland case. Your janitor is Frisco's problem, not ours. Take some deep breaths, and I'll call over there and set you up."

"Can we do it later, Perry? My Board is meeting in an hour, and if I'm not there, Dorothy'll turn me into a castrati."

"Castrato," Perry corrected me, showing off that megawatt smile of his at the same time. "What do you mean 'turn you into a castrati?' You don't even have the balls to take a day off when you need it! You should be in bed asleep! Have you had anything to eat?"

"A little ice cream."

"Get some real lunch and go to your damn meeting. But as soon as you get there, I want you to call SFPD and tell them who you are, and that you understand they're looking for you. Either that or they'll find you and pull you out of your meeting. I'm sure the Board would love to see that. Not to mention how Dorothy might respond to the arrest of her number one fundraiser."

"What about the dog?" I asked incongruously, as if to banish the thought from my mind.

"The dog doesn't have to say anything."

"I've got to get that dog some real dog food... Walk me to the car, Perry, I'll show him to you. JJ's phone number is on the dog tag, but I called. Nobody there."

# Chapter Eight

I thought about Perry's explanation for JJ's suicide – a doctor's diagnosis over the phone. The phone... Who speaks to their doctor at two in the morning? And that thought reminded me that it was close to two in the afternoon, and I had a Board meeting to attend, by order of the boss. I wanted only to sleep, but, while my desire continued, the reality of the situation made achieving it impossible, at least for now.

I drove home, deposited Pee-Pee, wolfed down a quart of Rocky Road, and then did exactly as Perry had insisted I do, and phoned the San Francisco Police Department. They wanted me there "right now," but I used those techniques I had acquired over years to part people from their money, and sweet-talked them into letting me show up after the Board meeting, as long as I got there by 4:00 p.m.

When I returned to my car for the drive back to San Francisco, I felt my stomach tighten. As the Datsun sputtered back into life, I thought again of the Bridge I was about to drive over, and froze. How long would these paralyzing episodes affect me? I forced myself to back down the driveway, but as I did, my hands again began to sweat, to the point that even gripping the steering wheel became an effort. I pulled the car back up to the top of the driveway, walked down the street, and caught the FX TransBay bus, which deposited me only two blocks from F.A.C.T.'s office.

I hated Board meetings at the best of times, and these were far from the best of times. I always felt like an actor who was afraid of forgetting his lines, but even more afraid of ad-libbing. Our Board of Directors was like any other, filled with two kinds of people: the ones who knew how to bring in the money, and the ones who were surrogates for the Director. The surrogates were free to say to staff what the Director was thinking but felt constrained to say out of fear of shattering the illusion that we were equal. "We are all just one big family" was the oft-repeated myth that all of us knew to be a myth, but which we all played along with. Today's meeting would require all my most tactical skills to keep me from breaking down altogether.

"Mr. Ovitz!" The voice pierced my drifting consciousness, and I snapped back into the present and the unmistakable voice of Reneé Cabrillo. Sitting at the foot of a long table in the Conference Room, I suddenly remembered where I was, and that I was being asked to give the Board a progress report on the upcoming fundraising banquet. To lose my place in this setting, to forget where I was and what I was doing, was to put my job at risk. Reporting to them is what they paid me to do.

"You were giving us an update on the benefit Dinner," the voice continued, "when you seemed to just drift off. For some reason, this most important event of the year seemed to be less important than whatever it was you were thinking about. Are you giving the Dinner the attention it deserves? I don't mean to be rude," she said, though she obviously did mean just that, "but you are certainly not giving us the attention we deserve!"

Ms. Cabrillo, as she insisted on being called, was the most obvious example of the outspoken, in-your-face Board member. She was Dorothy's alter ego on the Board, letting Dorothy appear to be the benign director, even when the villain was acting in Dorothy's stead. All the staff feared her, mostly because of the imperious way she thought of herself, as if she were the First Lady of the Philippines. If you looked up the word "haughty" in the dictionary, you would find a picture of Reneé Cabrillo! She had no ability to raise money, a job which fell principally to another Board member, Stanton McMullen. He never opened his mouth at a Board meeting (his best quality), but his career in banking made him uniquely qualified for his role as Board fundraiser.

Ms. Cabrillo's job, to put it as charitably as possible, was as gunslinger, which is precisely the role Dorothy had put her on the Board to play. She openly expressed the snooty nastiness that Dorothy had learned, over the years, to keep in check. Better to designate, to handpick a friend she could rely on to say out loud what Dorothy was thinking. As far as Ms. Cabrillo was concerned, I was nothing more than the hired help, and she never bothered even to try to disguise her feelings of superiority, plus a certain particular contempt for me, the reasons for which were never explained. I could only hope that Dorothy did not share that contemptuous feeling.

In a voice dripping with sarcasm, Ms. Cabrillo asked, "Do you mind terribly rejoining the Board meeting with the rest of us?" What I heard was, "Do you mind doing your job?"

I tried to clear my head. What time was it?

"Harrison," Dorothy herself prompted.

Before I could answer, Ms. Cabrillo took over Dorothy's thought and finished it, as she often did.

"I don't know what's the matter with you, but something clearly is. If the responsibilities of the Dinner are too much..." She let the phrase sit there, and I suddenly thought, *This must be what they mean by a dog doing its business*. Ms. Cabrillo had just done her business right there at the table, for maximum effect, and, strangely, as bad as it smelled, it cut through the shock, the sense of unreality I could not shake. Maybe that's because I took it exactly as she meant it – a literal wake-up call.

With my competency challenged and my ego attacked, my defense mechanisms went into high gear. "Ms. Cabrillo," I said as calmly, as sweetly as I could without sounding as phony as I felt, "you are perceptive as always." The flattery did nothing to change her attack mode. It never did. Nothing did. "There is something the matter with me. But it has nothing to do with the Dinner, I can assure you. The Dinner is going to be another great success."

"We have heard nothing so far to give us any assurances that is true, Mr. Ovitz," she said icily.

Like a doctor involved in a car crash, I went into professional mode. Without actually thinking about it, almost automatically, I reeled off all that I had done to ensure the Dinner would be the great success I had just promised the Board it would be. In fact, I had pretty much done all that had to be done to be able to make that promise. At this point, except for the inevitable loose ends that could and would be tied up by anyone working at the Foundation, the Dinner was on automatic pilot. I had no doubt it would land safely.

Still, like a kid painting by the numbers – a phrase I studiously avoided using – I gave them an impressive check list: The string trio from last year, "We Three Strings," would again provide the subdued background music; "We Cater to You" would provide three entrée choices, including a vegan "no-meat-meatloaf," which, to my surprise, had been the most popular choice the year before; they also promised that the dessert would "knock them off their chairs" – a flaming berry cobbler, à la mode if you wanted it, (and I wanted all the à la mode I could get); a 12-minute video of F.A.C.T.'s accomplishments, both over the life of its existence and, more particularly, of the past year; Serena Douglas and Ernest Calloway, now adults, would talk, separately and briefly, about their childhood abuse and the fact that F.A.C.T. had provided them both resources and a community in which to grow and feel whole again; and a number of other clients would provide intermittent entertainment, from humorous sketches to magic tricks, from solo singing to a rousing group of break dancers; finally, Dorothy would close the show with a short but pithy pitch for money (there were envelopes at every table); and a good time would be had by all.

Apparently, I had said all the right things. Various Board members smiled and nodded their approval, not at me but at Dorothy who put on a tight smile in return. I heard myself asking, "Are there any questions?"

Any questions? I had one. Why? Why did JJ decide that the answer to Hamlet's question was "not to be?" So many whys. Why then? Why there? He could not have known that traffic would stop on the Bridge. He could not have planned it, at least not like that. Had JJ planned to kill himself and simply seized the opportunity? When had he made that fateful decision?

"When you're ready, Harrison." It was the unfailingly pleasant Board member, Mimi Weston. Her young son had been abused by her ex-husband, his step-father, which made it impossible to keep her off the Board, though she filled neither the role of fundraiser nor of alter ego. She was uniquely herself, the one bright spot I could count on. Her eager face told me she was waiting for an answer to some question she had apparently posed, but which I had no memory of having heard.

"I'm so sorry, Mimi. Could you repeat that question?"

It was as if I were moving in and out of a trance. Did my own words, my own voice, have the power to hypnotize me, to take me out of the "now" and return me to the "then"? As soon as I said the words, "the question," another one popped into my head. I saw Soul Man, somber-faced and mute, listening to the disembodied voice at the other end of that line. Who was it? And what was it he said to make JJ jump?

Thoughts and images raced around my head, some of them rational. How many questions could I list, and can I now add "how many" to this list? Why, when, who, what, and now, how many? What am I forgetting?

"Where is your mind, Harrison?" It was sweet Mimi again, this time with genuine concern.

Dorothy was sitting at the head of the table, directly opposite me. Behind her on the wall was a large clock. I looked up and started to panic when I saw that it was already 3:40.

"I'm so sorry, but I have to go," I said, as if in answer to Mimi's question. Getting up from the table, I was vaguely aware of the mumbled reactions among the Board.

"What do you mean 'go'?" Dorothy and Ms. Cabrillo asked at the same time.

"I have to... I can't be late. The police are expecting me."

"The police!" Mimi said, startled. She wasn't the only one. I saw the shock on other faces as I turned to leave the room, and thought *they don't know what shock is.* I walked out of the Conference Room, into Audrey's reception space, and heard the sharp thwack of Ms. Cabrillo's voice behind me: "Mr. Ovitz! You get right back here!" That direct order almost succeeded; at least I paused for a moment, before continuing toward my rendezvous.

I winked at Audrey, who looked truly concerned, walked out of the office, and stepped into a waiting elevator. The questions I had trumped all of theirs. It was as simple as that. Dorothy could explain what she knew. She could smooth things over with the Board. Or not. I didn't care anymore. If I had to walk away now – and it looked like I might – at least no one could say that I had done a bad job. Strangely, that was still important to me.

The elevator disgorged me into the unexceptional lobby of our unexceptional building on 6th Street, around the corner from the so-called Hall of Justice. What a misnomer that is! You have money, you go in, pay what you need to pay, and walk out. You don't have money, you go in and stay in. The courts occupied the first two floors, but above them was the jail, which took up another three levels. This was also where the District Attorney maintained an office next to the police interrogators, which is where I was now heading, to be grilled like a cheese sandwich by "San Francisco's Finest." Perry had told me too much about his colleagues for me to believe that label, any more than I believed that justice was much in evidence at the Hall of Justice.

There was no escaping the ordeal that lay ahead of me any more than there was of escaping the ordeal that lay behind. Would I be able to walk out, like a person with money, or was I headed to jail? I just didn't know. I didn't know, either, whether I would I have a job to return to after my Board performance just now. The questions just wouldn't stop.

# Chapter Nine

I got through the metal detector at the Hall of Justice and went to the bank of elevators. Three of the four were out of order, and there was a crowd waiting in front of the one that worked, which was descending painfully slowly from the 5th floor. I decided to take the stairs to the 4th floor where the D.A. wanted to ask me "a few questions," as the Assistant D.A. had put it on the phone.

I walked up the stairs slowly, trying to anticipate the questions I'd be asked while still processing the questions I was asking myself. What could I tell them they didn't already know? What could they tell me I didn't already know?

As it turned out, each of us had something the other didn't know. But there was no way I could have known that as I continued my deliberate ascent.

As promised, I found the D.A.'s office on the 4th floor. His door looked exactly as I imagined it would look from the many TV cop shows I'd watched over the years; it had a pane of rough translucent glass at the top with the words DISTRICT ATTORNEY stenciled in bold black just above his name, Virgil G. Gresham.

The sergeant at the desk was expecting me, which I expected, but I wasn't expecting that he'd have a message for me. "Got a call from an officer in Oakland. Says he knows you," the sergeant said. Without looking up, he did a quick search of some paper piles stacked on his desk until he found what he was looking for.

"Wrote it down. Wanted to get it right," he said, in a voice that told me he was clearly skeptical of the claim that the caller was either a cop or a friend. He almost sneered as he read from the note, "'*Lilla wants you for dinner. Bring the stupid dog.*' That's it. No name. I asked, but he said you'd know."

The stupid dog! Would he die of starvation before I remembered to buy him dog food? I was pretty sure that a dog cannot live on ice cream alone. Ah, Pee-Pee. Stupid dog!

"Thank you, Sergeant," I said, managing a smile. "Should I sit here?" I pointed to a bench running down the length of one wall. And, judging from the initials, Roman numerals, and other identifying marks carved into the wood and its peeling brown paint, its usual occupants led more colorful lives than I did.

"No, Mr. Ovitz," the sergeant said. "Mr. Gresham would like you to go in now."

When I did, the first surprise that greeted me was LACE. Dressed for the occasion in a sleek black low-cut dress, she sat in a straight-back chair alongside the D.A.'s massive mahogany desk. Her shapely legs were crossed, and she wore black stiletto heels with a hint of green trim that matched the color of her earrings. *Dressed to kill*, I thought.

"That's him!" She almost screamed it, pointing an accusing finger that, like the rest of her, had been manicured and painted to be noticed. "That's him," she said again.

"Sit down, Mr. Ovitz," the D.A. said, ignoring LACE and motioning me to a chair facing him on the other side of that huge desk. I sat heavily, suddenly keenly aware of my precarious situation, while still reeling from feelings I couldn't fully understand. Seeing LACE put me back on that cold Bridge. I began to shiver.

"We have a witness here telling us that she saw you last night take something from the truck the jumper left on the Bridge. Is she right? Did you remove something, anything, from that truck?"

"That's him," LACE reiterated for the third time.

*The jumper*, I thought. That was the brand name of my sister's jump rope in elementary school. The Jumper. It could have been a piece of clothing, a new style. It could have been many things, but hearing it applied to the man whose eyes met mine made my hands sweat.

"I need you to answer my question, Mr. Ovitz. Unless you feel the need to have an attorney present. That is certainly your right." Another reminder that this was not a game, and that I needed to pay attention. I knew this last reminder was intended to goad me into talking against my own best interests, but I had already determined that my own best interests were in telling the D.A. exactly what had happened.

"I have nothing to hide," I said quickly, "but perhaps, if I'm facing some sort of criminal charge..."

"See!" LACE said it in triumph. "I told you!"

The D.A. began the familiar warning, "If there is evidence you committed a crime, you have the right to remain silent because..."

"...whatever you say can and will be used against you," LACE said, finishing the phrase she'd memorized from the countless TV arrests she'd witnessed.

Gresham pressed a button on his phone, and the front-desk Sergeant knocked twice, then entered the room.

"I'd like you to escort our witness to the cafeteria and have them treat her to whatever she likes," the D.A. instructed, before turning his attention to LACE. "That's our thanks for the valuable identification and information you have provided. Thank you, again. We will contact you as the need arises."

LACE seemed satisfied with her payoff, and followed the sergeant out of the room.

"So, what's it gonna be," the D.A. asked as soon as the door closed behind them. "The truth, if you have nothing to hide, and a story, if you lawyer up." He smiled in the way a fox might smile at a chicken.

"Okay, okay," I clucked, exhaling a long-held sigh. "I get the idea. Here's what happened." I told him the whole story, leaving nothing out, including LACE's impatient honking for traffic to get moving, and the pot-smoking teen in the BMW behind me. The D.A. raised his eyebrows a little when I got to the part about taking Pee-Pee and the wet note from the floor of the pick-up, but otherwise, his face revealed no reaction. Nothing. And then, finally, a smile.

"We've spoken with the driver of the ice cream truck. His story matches yours. By the way, what was on the note?" I told him, and about the conversation with JJ's former employer.

"And the dog?"

The stupid dog. "He's waiting for me right now at home. I haven't even had time to feed him."

"Better go do that, then," the D.A. said. "We may have more questions for you at a later date, so don't leave town without asking."

"Is that it?" I asked, relieved. "You're not putting me in jail?"

"By the way," he continued, "did you happen to get a look at the license plate on that kid's BMW? Any part of the number you can remember? We'd like to talk to him, too."

"If I did, subsequent memories wiped it out," I said.

"What do you suppose prompted him to do it," the D.A. asked.

After a few moments of silence, I tried to give an answer. "I've thought about it," I began. "In fact, that's all I've been thinking about since... All I can come up with is it had to be related to the phone call."

"Phone call? What phone call? You didn't say anything about a phone call."

Besides a sudden fear that I may no longer be safe from prosecution, I was shocked at my own oversight. I hadn't forgotten, exactly, I had just started telling the story at the point where JJ stepped down from the pick-up's cab. I don't know why I started it there. My mind wasn't working right.

"Oh, yeah," I said, trying to sound matter-of-fact. "I forgot to tell you that."

I was aware that the D.A. was now looking at me as if I were a suspect, though I wasn't sure what crime I was suspected of committing. "Is that all you forgot to tell me," he asked, then added, "Words have consequences."

*So do the absence of words*, I thought. "No. Nothing else. I'm sorry. I'm very tired. I just forgot," I tried assuring him with as much confidence as I could muster. "Nothing else. He was on the car phone, but he wasn't talking. He was listening. Then he stepped out of the truck. I told you everything else. I just forgot."

Whether he believed I had just forgotten or not, Gresham relaxed. "Now that's something we didn't know," he said, nodding his head appreciatively. "That's something we might be able to track." And then, as if an afterthought, or by way of telling me I'd passed his trust test, he said, "Oh, yes. There's something I forgot to tell you, too. We fished the jumper out of the Bay this morning. He washed up around China Basin. Wasn't wearing any pants. Probably ripped off by the wind on the way down, or pulled off by the current. Anyway, we know it's him from the descriptions you and the other witnesses gave us. No other ID on him, obviously."

They had his body. I hadn't known that before. And knowing it had the same effect on me as hearing Soul Man reduced to "the Jumper." His body! I had seen his body in full animated motion. I had seen him move deliberately, purposefully, between my car and LACE's. I had shared some strange intimacy with him through our eyes, alive and full of passion. He was a man. Over the past twelve hours or so, that is the only way I had pictured him. Now, suddenly, that image of warm-blooded life morphed into its antithesis: a piece of meat. A body. Dead.

"We were hoping his wallet would unlock some secrets," Gresham added, waking me from my reverie. "We're hoping his employer, uh, that is his former employer, might help us locate next of kin. You can't help us with that, can you?"

"I wish I could. I honestly do. I can't seem to let go of Mr. Jeppards. Or, maybe it's him that won't let go of me."

"This is a matter for the police, Mr. Ovitz. For the moment, I'm satisfied you haven't committed a crime I care to charge you with, although you have to know that taking that dog and that note from the jumper's truck was tampering with evidence."

"But I didn't know..." I started to explain.

"Forget it. I'm just saying..."

I thanked him for the not-so-subtle warning, promised I wouldn't try to interfere with the police business, and retraced my steps back down the staircase to the first floor.

I walked up to Market Street to catch BART back to Oakland. The train screeched to a stop, and I boarded a very full car. I squeezed into a window seat next to an obese man sitting in the aisle seat, and pulled out the note the sergeant had written – scrawled, really – to record Perry's exact words: "Lilla wants you for dinner." Hah! "And bring the stupid dog."

By the time I got home, Pee-Pee had lived up to his name. There was a large puddle on the floor in front of the back door that he had already learned led to the garden. I looked at Pee-Pee, who lowered his head, and my heart melted. Like a child made to hold his or her urine, providing the pretext for the torturer to "punish" the offender – a scenario far too familiar at F.A.C.T. – Pee-Pee shivered and looked ashamed.

"You poor thing," I reassured the trembling dog. I lifted the pitiful little mutt into my arms and carried him out, putting him onto the small patch of garden. Pee-Pee sniffed, found a suitable spot, and, with near-audible relief, he relieved himself, first of number two, then, again of number one.

"Let's get you something to eat," I said. One of those random thoughts ricocheted across my brain. Could a person who called himself Soul Man be capable of abusing an animal? I chose to think not.

I put an old towel on the floor where Pee-Pee had widdled, and left it there as I walked across the street to the Safeway. Pee-Pee was just as excited to see me return five minutes later as he had been a few minutes earlier when I got back from San Francisco. I brought him a bag of dry dog food and four varieties of the canned stuff. I didn't know what the little worm liked, but I knew he had to be hungry. I was hungry.

I filled two bowls, one with kibble and the other with a lamb and rice stew mix from one of the cans, and was surprised by how delicately the little dog went at both, eating a little from one, then switching to the other. While he did that, I listened to a message from Audrey on my answer machine. Apparently, Ms. Cabrillo had demanded that I be fired on the spot for "insubordination." Dorothy had pacified her, at least temporarily, but, Audrey warned, "you're skating on thin ice, Harry, and you could just strike out." I loved how Audrey routinely mixed her metaphors. It was too late to call Dorothy now, and, anyway, I wasn't sure what I would say. My job seemed the least important thing in my life right now.

Sleep was the most important thing. And I tried. I had another hour or so before dinner at Perry and Lilla's, and I lay down. Pee-Pee settled comfortably on the bed beside me, and immediately went to sleep. But, as much as I wanted it, I could not follow his example. Maybe I was just too tired to sleep. Instead, my stomach rumbled, reminding me, as if I needed reminding, that Lilla wanted me for dinner. That meant I was going to eat real food tonight. She was an absolutist about that. The first time I came for dinner, she had said, "Ice cream! Shit! Ice cream is dessert. I'll serve it after dinner."

That is what I was thinking of when, twenty minutes later, I awoke with a start. Pee-Pee was licking my face. I had just enough time to shave and shower before Lilla would start to get angry, ready with one of her lectures whenever I was late. Tonight, I was determined not to be. "To be or not to be?" There it was again.

"Not to be late," I said to Pee-Pee, who had by now finished the bowl of dry food and was working on the bowl of stew. "C'mon, Boy," I said, scooping him up. "We've got a date."

# Chapter Ten

I drove carefully, obeying all the traffic laws, more fearful of cops than I had ever been. Or, maybe I was more fearful of everything than I had ever been. Pee-Pee curled up on the front seat beside me. "I hate to say it," I said, "but you're a comforting little worm." And he was.

Perry lived in a part of town that was gentrifying so fast, that the modest three-bedroom bungalow he had bought for just under $150,000 two years before was now valued at close to half a million. I was, of course, very happy for him, but wondered idly why such things never happened to me. Another example of the fact that I couldn't seem to transfer my fundraising skills to my own life. Oh well.

I arrived at Perry's door with Pee-Pee tucked securely under my arm. Perry opened the door. He was wearing an apron covering a well-pressed but casual blue Polo shirt and half covering a pair of jeans that he had ironed to perfection. The apron itself, with its little red fish sporting huge smiling lips, contrasted sharply with the crisp look it covered. Perry's smile, as broad as those on his apron's little fishes, seemed to cast as bright a light as the bulb over the door, as he announced in a voice loud enough for the neighbors to hear, "Oh, good! The felon has arrived! And he brought the pooch."

The pooch's ears had perked up at the labored strains of *Für Elise* coming from inside the house, that Beethoven piece that all beginning piano students learn at some point along the way. Judging by how she was mangling the chords, seven-year-old Ayusha was not that far along the way. This was all part of Lilla's plan, I knew. She had mapped out her children's futures, including their music lessons (which four-year-old Sasha had also just begun). She insisted that they become fluent in at least one other language, leaving them to choose which language to study, a regimen to begin before they were out of elementary school. They would both be given rigorous tutoring in preparation for university and careers in a profession. Whenever I teased Lilla about the control she tried to exert over their lives and futures, she would say, "Well, I'm not telling them which profession. They're free to choose." But freedom had its limits; choose they must. I often wondered how my life might have been different if I had had such a mother, instead of the wonderfully crazy one I did have.

Besides the battered Beethoven in the air, there was a delicious aroma wafting through the door past Perry and tantalizing my nostrils and taste buds, and I was ready for the feast I knew would follow. Among his many other talents, Perry was a heck of a cook.

"Lilla," Perry called to his wife, "c'mere and look at this." He was laughing, and I found myself feeling slightly defensive. Surprisingly, I realized it wasn't me, but Pee-Pee I felt protective of.

The labored strains of *Für Elise* came to a brief halt as Lilla came to the door. Over her shoulder, she shouted "Ayusha. Keep it up," and the familiar piece began again from the beginning. Lilla looked me up and down, as she always did, as if deciding whether I passed muster or not (I always expected her to ask to see my hands to make sure I had washed for dinner), and then fixed her stare on Pee-Pee, the first time she had laid eyes on him. She reached out to the little rat, who instantly licked her hand. She patted him gently, looked at Perry and nodded approvingly. *What is this about,* I wondered.

"Sasha. Ayusha," she shouted into the space behind her. "I want you to see something."

Sasha was right behind her. She came to her mother's side and asked, "What?"

"You told me to practice," Ayusha called from another room.

"And now I'm telling you to come here. There's something you're gonna wanna see, I promise," Lilla called back to her older daughter. In a minute, both beautiful girls were standing between their parents and me.

"Look," Lilla said, pointing to Pee-Pee.

Ayusha saw him first. "Ohhh," she said, stretching the word for so long she seemed to deflate as the air left her body. Then she reinflated and continued oohing and ahhing in obvious delight. Somewhere around Ayusha's third intake of breath, Sasha finally focused in on my little dog. When she saw Pee-Pee, she instantly turned to her mother – not her father, I noted – and asked, "Can we keep her? Huh? Can we?"

"Well, first of all," Lilla corrected, "it's a he, not a she, a him not a her. And second of all, he is not mine, so I cannot give him to you."

"Ohhh," came Ayusha's instant reaction. This time it did not have the excited high-pitched tone of her first outburst. This time her voice came in a lower register, its falling intonation a clear expression of disappointment.

Sasha was undeterred. "Whose is it," she asked her mother.

"Uncle Harrison's," Lilla said, looking straight into my eyes. I suddenly realized that despite Lilla's apparent role as commander-in-chief, this was Perry's doing, Perry-the-Fixer. He had orchestrated this little scene, and there was method to his madness. I was merely an instrument in Perry's orchestra, an instrument he was able to play far better than Ayusha's piano piece.

"Well, not exactly," I said, cutting in. "The police told me today that I could be charged with the crime of withholding evidence." I crouched to the girls' level and asked, "Do you want to know what evidence I was withholding?"

"What," Sasha asked eagerly.

"This stupid dog," I answered.

"He is not stupid," Ayusha chimed in. "He's smart. He's a good dog!" She said it with certainty, as if that were the last word on the matter.

"And Daddy's the police," Sasha reminded us. "Daddy can wiffhold evidence," she added, not quite understanding what those words meant. "Can't you Daddy? Can't you wiffhold evidence." It came out more as a plea than a question.

"With, not wiff," Ayusha corrected her sister, pointedly making sure to stick her tongue out dramatically.

"Ayusha!" Lilla said. There was a sharpness in her voice that surprised me. Ayusha looked down, and said, "I'm sorry."

Perry pretended to think about Sasha's question. "Well," he said to both his daughters, "I can't really withhold evidence..."

"Yes you can, Daddy! Yes you can!" Sasha argued.

"Let me finish, Sweet Pea," he continued. "I was saying that I can't withhold evidence, but I can hold evidence."

Without understanding exactly what the words meant, Sasha understood what Perry was telling her, and she squealed. Ayusha joined her sister's excited anticipation, and I found myself looking into the wide eyes of two very hopeful children.

Suddenly, I was aware of just how attached to this little dog I had become in so short a time. Without trying, he had charmed his way into my heart, and I was shocked by the realization. My first instinct was to hold Pee-Pee even closer to my side, even while I realized what a perfect solution Perry was offering me. I could relinquish possession of this "evidence" into the hands of the police, while giving the two special children in my life what they wanted most in the world at this moment. Perry knew long before I did that the same heart that had melted like ice cream at Pee-Pee's antics would melt even more in the presence of his daughters' overwhelming desire.

With a pang, I put the dog down and, as he had done when I brought him home, he ran past the four Ely's who stood in the doorway and into the house, as if he'd always lived there. Two squealing little girls were in hot pursuit.

"C'mon in," Perry said, a father's proud smile on his face. Lilla nodded, and retreated into the house, hoping to resume supervising her daughter's practice session. But with this new addition to the household, that possibility apparently was not to be.

"Galldernit," I said. "I just bought dog food for the stupid dog." I chuckled as I said it, more to cover my unexpected emotional response to losing Pee-Pee than for any other reason.

"Never mind, Harrison," Perry said. "I'll pick it up later. You know this is the best solution, don't you? You can see how much they already love him, can't you? And you have visitation rights whenever you want."

And, in truth, I knew he was right. The police warning was only one reason why giving Pee-Pee up was the prudent thing to do. There was also the fact that I worked all the time, was hardly ever home, had a major fundraiser ahead of me, and would never be able to lavish the attention that Sasha and Ayusha were already showing the little mutt. And when I saw them playing with him (*dog tag*, I thought), chasing him from room to room and then running from him as he chased them from room to room, I smiled. For the very first time, I heard him bark, a quick series of high-pitched yips, sometimes drowned out by the sound of little girl laughter. Pee-Pee was in heaven. The house was warm with cooking, and now I was warm too.

With the children preoccupied with their game of dog tag, Lilla joined Perry and me in the kitchen. She offered to assist her husband's dinner preparations, as I did, but Perry rejected all offers of help. He had already set the table, so Lilla grabbed a couple of Coronas from the fridge, popped them open, set one down in front of me, and took the chair next to me at the table. I loved this little room because it was all-purpose: cooking, eating, conversing. Living.

Perry opened the oven door and removed a beautifully browned pork roast whose aroma filled the room. As if an afterthought, he said, "Oh yeah, I learned something today you might be interested in." Perry-the-Fisherman, baiting his hook.

"What? Something about JJ," I asked, hooked.

"Maybe," Perry teased.

"Okay," I said after that first satisfying swig of beer, "what's this interesting news?"

"Dinner first," Perry said, with a wink. Lilla called the girls to the table.

At that moment, Pee-Pee came tearing into the room and squatted under the table where both girls attempted to follow him.

"That's enough," Lilla said. "Time to settle down. It's time for dinner."

"Uncle Harrison," Sasha said. "What's his name?"

Perry and Lilla exchanged a resigned look, shook their heads, and looked at me.

"Pee-Pee," I said, setting both girls off into fits of laughter, which quickly rubbed off on the so-called adults in the room, until Lilla regained control.

"It's time to take Pee-Pee to your room and close the door. Then you two can go pee-pee and wash your hands for dinner." I thought she might ask me to do the same, but she didn't.

"Oooh, Mommy said a bad word," Sasha scolded.

"No, I didn't," Lilla replied. "That's just your new dog's name." The girls giggled. "Now go do what I told you."

Perry bent down and scooped Pee-Pee up and handed him to Sasha. Still giggling, two happy sisters carried one happy dog to their room.

"So," I said, turning to Perry.

But before he could tell me what he had found, the girls came back into the kitchen and took their seats.

"Enough talk for now," Lilla said. She spoke to the children, but she was actually addressing us. "Cut the roast," she instructed Perry, who shrugged in my direction and did as he was told. As he cut dinner-sized slices of pork roast at the kitchen counter, Lilla put a beautiful arugula salad in the middle of the table. She doled out a scoop of mashed sweet potatoes onto the girls' plates before setting the bowl down on the table for me to serve myself. Perry put a platter of the sliced roast next to the potatoes, and sat down. Lilla examined the table, her daughters, her guest and her husband before sitting. Talk of police business was banned at meals whenever the children were present, so we talked of other things: what Ayusha was learning in school, what Sasha liked most about her pre-school teacher, Lilla's latest case at the Public Defender's office where she plied her legal training and liberal leanings, and, of course, all things relating to Pee-Pee.

Perry served up one of his specialties for dessert. He called it ABC pie even though there was nothing elementary about it, and it wasn't pie. It was acai-boysenberry-cobbler, still warm from the oven, and topped with Vanilla Freeze ice cream that immediately began to melt from the warmth. But Perry's culinary craft was lost on me; I was too preoccupied with whatever it was he wanted to tell me about JJ to truly enjoy the confection. The girls gulped their desserts down, and begged to go back to their room to play with their new dog.

"Okay," Lilla allowed, "but you still have to finish practicing," she said to Ayusha, though we all knew that wasn't going to happen. And the girls were gone.

I saw them once more before I left for home. I peeked into their room all by myself to see both girls sound asleep, Sasha in her bed and Ayusha on the rug with her arm draped over Pee-Pee sleeping beside her. I knew this was the best solution both for Pee-Pee and for the two little girls who would adore him. No question about that. So why was I feeling so torn? For one thing, of course, the little worm had wormed his way into my heart. But there was something else, too: a twinge of guilt. *Guilt for what*, I wondered. Guilt for not holding Soul Man back from his fearful flight into oblivion? Guilt for revealing my fear of him before he threw himself into the Bay? Guilt for taking his dog and now giving him up, and losing the only tangible connection I had to JJ? Whatever the cause, the feeling slipped away as I saw the three of them sleeping there.

"You're a terrible criminal," Perry whispered behind me, as I closed their bedroom door.

"What's that supposed to mean," I asked.

"I'll tell you after we do the dishes. C'mon."

Lilla had already cleared the table. I volunteered to do the washing. It was the one household task I loved. It was so satisfying to start with a sink of messy dishes and end with those same dishes, now sparkling clean and stacked neatly in the dish rack. Perry picked up a towel, and dried the dishes as fast as I could stack them.

"I heard you had some problems with your Board meeting today," Lilla said, from the table where she was nursing a cup of hot tea. "Don't lose your job, Harrison," she added, waving a finger in my direction. "We can't afford to keep you!"

Perry and I finished washing and drying, and I still had not heard what Perry had learned. "What did you mean when you said I was a terrible criminal," I asked again, as Perry put away the last dish.

"Get your good-bye kiss from Lilla, and I'll tell you," he teased.

"You're beginning to pith me off," I said.

Perry and Lilla walked me to the door, where I waited for his explanation. I had to repeat my question. "For the third time, what did you mean by that?"

"Just this," he said. "You took a note and a dog from Soul Man's truck, but you missed a significant piece of evidence in the glove compartment..."

I waited.

"I talked to a friend of mine over there at the SFPD," he continued, "and guess what they found?"

I waited.

Lilla jumped in, as impatient as I was to dislodge whatever it was that Perry knew. "If somebody doesn't talk," she said, feigning anger, "somebody is not going to get breakfast, among other things somebody's not going to get!"

"A VFW membership card," Perry said without further prompting.

"Which means?"

"Which means he was a member of the local VFW, so there are people who knew him that we should talk to. The cops haven't even been able to find where he lived yet because the home address he gave his employer was false. So, maybe someone there can tell us. Maybe they can tell us why he did what he did."

My fundraising responsibilities, my job itself, seemed to vanish from my thoughts. Now, the only thing I could think of was talking to people who knew JJ. I wanted to know what they knew. I wanted to know everything about him.

"When can we meet them," I asked.

"Well, being the superior investigator that I am," Perry said with another wink, "I checked it out. The chapter he belonged to is hosting a potluck dinner Tuesday night. I'll make a pot of beans. You can bring ice cream."

"You mean crashing their dinner party?"

"V! F! W!" Perry enunciated each letter as if he were speaking to a child, or someone whose first language was not English. "Veterans of Foreign Wars. I am a veteran of foreign wars," Perry reminded me. "I kicked Noriega's butt out of Panama and Saddam Hussein's butt out of Kuwait."

"Ain't war great," I said. "Have gun, will travel."

With his signature brilliant smile, he nodded in my direction and replied, "Have small gun, will travel damn little!"

"Very funny," I said. "So I guess doing what you're ordered to do makes you a hero."

"Damn straight! I'm a true American hero! If that's not VFW material, I don't know what is. I'm entitled, and I'm entitled to bring a guest."

"What'll they say when two strangers show up?"

"I guess we'll find out on Tuesday."

I kissed Lilla goodnight, returned to my empty house, and fell into a deep, dreamless sleep.

# Chapter Eleven

I woke early, stumbled out of bed, and was halfway to the kitchen to get Pee-Pee some breakfast before I remembered that he was now in more competent hands than mine. That realization, however comforting for Pee-Pee, didn't prepare me for the surge of sadness I felt. *When this is all over*, I thought, *I might get myself a dog.*

I made a pot of coffee, spooned out a bowl of passion fruit sorbet for breakfast, and left for work.

The office felt different – or maybe the office was the same and I was different. Because of my abrupt departure from the Board meeting, Audrey was particularly solicitous, as if I might have a complete mental meltdown if she didn't keep asking me how I was. For the next few days, all I could think about was the VFW potluck Perry and I planned to crash. Even Dorothy seemed uncharacteristically concerned, asking how I was feeling when she arrived, usually a couple of hours after Audrey and I did, and an hour or so before the rest of her staff got there. Before the Harrison-Insults-the-Board-of-Directors Show, she would typically go straight to her office, nodding curtly to Audrey as she did. Now, she made a point of detouring to my office after her entrance, sticking her head in the doorway and asking, "How are you today, Harrison?" It was only days before the Big Dinner, and she was walking on eggshells.

"I'm okay," I lied.

I wasn't okay. I was obsessed, and not with work. Work became my way of getting through the day, while I counted the hours until our upcoming encounter with the people who actually knew JJ.

The Benefit Dinner was my salvation. It forced me to concentrate on real tasks that had to be completed. Most I could and did delegate, but some I had to handle myself, like speaking to the Mayor to schedule his short talk to the assembled guests, and to learn how many of his staff would be in attendance. As it turned out, the Mayor himself would be out of the country for the event, which I took as a blessing. It meant that my staff would not have to engage in the ego-stroking I had been pushing on them, and it freed up five minutes or so for the program. The Mayor had complained, not at last year's Benefit Dinner, but at the one before that. Someone – mercifully identified as one of the wait-staff and not a F.A.C.T. staff member – had failed to ask his entrée choice before serving him, and, much worse, had referred to him by his name rather than his title. He had snapped at the poor waitress, "You can call me His Honor or Mr. Mayor! Do not refer to me as Mr. Ingersoll!" The server turned bright red, and retreated to the kitchen in tears as soon as she could.

I checked each day's tasks off a list like an intern afraid of making a mistake. With each passing day, my mind focused less and less on the work I was paid to do and more and more on Tuesday's VFW potluck.

On Tuesday morning, I could think of nothing else. When Dorothy poked her head in to ask her now ritual question, I was so obsessed with that night's upcoming event, I failed to respond at all. She had to ask again.

"Harrison," she huffed, "I asked you how you are."

"Just thinking about the Benefit," I lied. "I'm fine."

"You're not fine," was her ominous reply. "You're not fine at all."

I smiled up at her, hoping that would ease her concern, but she had already turned her back and was walking away. The moment she disappeared into her office, Audrey came into mine.

"Oh, Harry," she said, "I'm so worried about you. She's been on the phone with Ms. Cabrillo, and that just can't be good. Please, please be careful, Harry."

But careful was no longer an option. The truth was that I already was too far into it – whatever "it" turned out to be – and there was no way I could extricate myself.

Perry and I had agreed to meet in front of the VFW Hall at 8:00 p.m. The dinner, we knew, would start half an hour earlier, so we timed our late entrance for maximum effect. We wanted them to be curious, to want to know who we were, to ask us questions so that we could start asking our own.

I had expected a bunch of men standing around a dark basement somewhere, drinking beer. Instead, the room was not only well lit, but three long tables covered in white butcher paper ran its length, and were almost completely occupied. American flags interspersed among the various military service flags were posted around the perimeter. A few women sat at the tables among the men on folding chairs, either veterans themselves or wives. They were smart enough to know what too many men did not: that stuffing their now more corpulent bodies into former military uniforms made them look ridiculous.

As it turned out, 8:00 wasn't late enough to make us stand out. People kept bringing in soft drinks, potato chips, salads and desserts for at least half an hour after we got there. Perry put his pot of black beans and sausage on the table between two different kinds of potato salad, one smothered in an unappetizing-looking red sauce. I asked an older man in Army uniform who seemed to be in charge where I could put the vanilla ice cream I'd brought, and he directed me through a door into a small kitchen. The refrigerator, stocked with Bud and Bud Lite – none of it available in the dining room – had a tiny freezer, which could barely accommodate the half gallon container.

We filled our plates from the table where Perry had placed his beans. I had downed a quart of Rocky Road before coming, so I put a few veggies on my plate, while Perry piled his high with fried chicken, potato salad, and a sampling of other dishes. He balanced a second plate that he filled with two unrecognizable desserts, and various cookies, as if they might not be there when he returned for seconds. *How is it that he can eat like that and still look as good as he does?* A random thought.

There were not two unoccupied chairs together, so Perry put himself at one table between two older men, perhaps JJ's contemporaries, while I found a place two tables away, on the end. The guy next to me was much younger than Perry's seatmates, and was dressed in civilian clothes. I felt completely out of my depth, but I could hear the ever-sociable Perry already introducing himself. I followed suit, introducing myself to the wrinkled old African American man in the ill-fitting uniform across the table from me and to the woman sitting next to him. The old geezer resumed his on-going argument with the woman. He was defending himself against some perceived anniversary offense. *Married for sure*, I concluded. He was about JJ's age, sported a neat, graying Afro, and looked like someone whom JJ might have befriended. I wanted to ask him what he knew, but before I found a convenient break in the subdued argument, the young white man sitting next to me spoke, and I turned my attention to him.

His T-shirt revealed both his toned upper body and a tempest of tattoos that covered both his arms. One tattoo, a snake-like rope, rose from beneath the shirt and encircled his neck like a prehensile tail, and my imagination went into high gear picturing what it was attached to underneath.

"Haven't seen you here before," he said, curious but friendly. "Is this your first time?"

"It is," I said, "but I'm not a veteran of any wars, foreign or domestic, so I don't really belong here."

He motioned toward Perry, two tables away. "How 'bout your friend? He a veteran?"

"How observant," I said, surprised that he had noted our entrance.

"I keep my eyes open," he replied. "I like to know who's around me."

"Yeah, he's a veteran," I said.

"You two a couple?"

"No! No! Of course not," I answered quickly, embarrassed by the question. "We're friends. But we're here for a purpose."

"I'm Rick," he said, offering his hand.

"Harrison," I said. "My friend's name's Perry."

"So, what mission are you and Perry on?"

I plunged in. "We're looking to find out all we can about a member of this VFW Post. Or, rather, he was a member before jumping off the Bay Bridge last week."

"You're talking about old Mr. Jeppards?"

My God! He knew JJ! All my senses came alive, and I was aware that my heart had begun to beat faster. My hands were probably sweating – I wasn't paying any attention to them – but if so, it was no longer out of shock or guilt, but anticipation. I was feeling a sense of excitement entirely different from the excitement that fear induces. I felt a surge of pride that it was I who had unearthed whatever it was Rick was about to tell me.

"You knew him?" I struggled to keep my voice as matter-of-fact as possible, to keep my rising excitement under control.

"Not much," Rick shrugged. "Better than most, though. Old Jeppards didn't talk much. Not to them, anyway." He nodded in the direction of the men, Black and white, all around us. "Didn't like to talk to the old men who fought the Big One, even though he was one of them. He talked to me, but he never really opened up."

For a second, he looked puzzled, as if he were trying to remember something. Then he refocused. "He kinda kept to hisself. But what's your interest? Are you cops?"

"Actually, Perry is a cop," I said, "but that has nothing to do with why we're here.

"Which is?"

Once more, I had to launch myself into the retelling. I had been waiting for it to become a rote process, words that convey a thought without any thinking behind them. But that time had not yet come. As before, the moment came rushing back, and again I found myself shivering in a cold fog, afraid. "I was in the car next to him that night," I explained, trying to keep the tremor out of my voice, but failing. "I watched him get out of his pick-up, and he watched me. Then..." Once again, my voice caught on the word that would finish the sentence, and finish JJ "...he jumped."

"Shit!" Rick said, looking at me squarely for the first time. "Wow!"

"I don't know anything else about him. Nothing. I... I... I know he worked as a janitor and owned a little dog, but that's it. That's all I know."

"More'n me, man," Rick said. "I didn't know that about him."

The women were clearing off the tables, carefully putting leftovers aside for whoever had brought them, and stacking empty dishes for the all-woman kitchen detail. Someone had brought out the ice cream, and put it on the table with the other desserts, now surrounded by men getting fatter. The couple on the other side of the table stopped their argument long enough to fill two paper plates with what looked like a little of everything – cherry pie, apple pie, pecan pie, and half a dozen Oreos. Oh yes, and for the gentleman, an extra-large serving of vanilla ice cream melting on both pieces of store-bought chocolate cake he was now devouring.

The din of the conversation all around made hearing difficult anyway, but now Rick lowered his voice to the point where I had to lean in just to hear him.

"I can tell you this," he practically whispered. "He served time in Leavenworth Federal Penitentiary."

I must have gasped at that, though I can't quite remember. Just that Rick was laughing at my response. "How..." I began, not knowing where that question wanted to go. I wanted to jump up, like Archimedes, and scream, *Eureka.* I wanted to hug this veteran of one of our more recent military adventures, like Perry. I quelled these impulses, and tried not to let my voice betray my desperate need to know all that he knew. "Not much," Rick had said, leading me to the edge of what that was.

"We were drunk," he chuckled, again. "The only time I ever got drunk with anyone here, and the only time he got drunk with anyone here. It just sorta happened. He showed up at a meeting here, and that almost never happened. He grabbed his chair and pulled it up next to me, don't ask me why. And he looked terrible."

"What do you mean he looked terrible?"

"He just didn't look good," Rick continued. "Completely distracted by something. And whatever it was, it had nothin' to do with the meeting. Anyway, he had this look. All I can say, it was a disturbed look. Yeah. Disturbed. So I asked him if he wanted to go up the street to get a drink. Never happened before."

"What's up the street?" By now, Rick was rolling, and my lame questions only slowed him down. But I was getting goose bumps listening to the story unfold, so maybe I needed him to slow down. I felt on the verge of something, and it pulled me forward, straining to hear his every word over the din, yet afraid. Of what? Of making some sense out of JJ's last act, while I sat in my car as his audience? Or was I just afraid of going over the edge myself?

"So we went to the bar," Rick continued, ignoring my inane question.

"What happened at the bar?" I finally managed to ask, ration-ally, back from the brink.

"He got drunk. We got drunk. Straight bourbon. Goes right to the head. Didn't calm him down at all. He started talking about going to prison for what happened at Port Chicago. That he was some kind of federal prisoner because he wouldn't carry explosives onto a ship after they already exploded once."

"What was he talking about?" *This could be it*, I thought. *There has to be a connection.*

"You never heard of Port Chicago?"

"Yeah, I've heard of it. It's where some veteran got run over by a Navy train a few years ago, right?"

"You gotta go back a lot longer than that. According to Mr. Jeppards," Rick said, "a bunch of Black sailors got blown up carrying ammunition, and when some of the survivors refused orders to follow in their bloody footsteps, they were court-martialed, and sent to Leavenworth."

"Had you ever heard of it before? Is it true?"

"Not much interested in military history," Rick said, "so I never followed up. But I believed him. Know what he told me? He said they didn't mind being used as mules, but they'd be asses if they obeyed." He chuckled at the memory of JJ's pun, adding with a laugh, "Said they'd be damned if they'd allow themselves to be used as asses."

"Did he say why it suddenly bothered him so much after so many years? What was he so distracted about? Did he tell you that?" I was surprised that I was back in control of my faculties. I was thinking straight, and asking good questions. I was learning some amazing things.

"I told you we were drunk. I don't remember too much. Something about a phone call he had. He was mixing up the two stories, the going to prison story with the phone call. He was pretty disturbed about that call."

"Who was he talking to? Did he say?"

"No idea. All I remember is he kept saying he served his country and went to prison for it."

I was suddenly aware that Perry was standing behind me. He had heard this last comment, and was respectfully riveted where he stood, hoping Rick would remember more details. He knew not to interfere when another investigator was getting good information from his source.

He knew, but still could not resist asking from behind me, "When did this happen?"

"Oh, excuse me," I said, getting up. "This is my friend, Perry Ely. Perry, this is Rick."

He looked up at Perry. "You the cop?"

"That's right," Perry replied amicably. Rick stood, turned, and walked out the door without another word.

"Sorry," I began, but Perry cut me off.

"It's happened before. I don't take it personally."

"I learned a thing or three," I announced proudly. "You?"

"Oh yeah," Perry said. "I learned a new recipe for potato salad. Let's get out of here, and you can fill me in."

"Could be the jackpot," I said, still proud of myself for learning what the professional had failed to learn. "If I could just figure out how these new pieces of the puzzle fit together."

I reminded Perry to collect his bean pot, which he did. We walked outside into an unusually warm December night. Perry motioned toward the red, white and blue neon sign up the street blinking Pat's Pub. "You can tell me what those pieces are over a beer," he said.

# Chapter Twelve

After telling Perry all that Rick had told me – "debriefing" Perry called it – we agreed to divvy up our tasks. I would learn as much as I could about what had happened at Port Chicago, and Perry would use his cop connections to get JJ's prison records.

The next couple of days felt like I had stepped into another world, even if most of those steps had happened while I was sitting. Sitting and reading. If any part of what Rick had told me over the din of dinner at the VFW were true, I was embarrassed that I knew nothing about it.

What I did know about – my paid work – I now felt only a tenuous connection to, compared to my newfound connection to Soul Man. How very strange. Especially, since I knew that my boss would not take this disconnection as worthy of discussion. There'd be no discussion. It would end before it began with her patented "End of discussion!"

With Rick's revelation of the night before still fresh, I phoned Audrey at home early the next morning. I told her I wouldn't be in that day.

"You sick?" she asked, concerned.

"No."

A long silence followed, as Audrey waited for an explanation I could not provide. I had none. Except a burning need to know what had happened to Mr. Jeppards. What had JJ done that led him to federal prison, and, I was sure, to that terrible end I wished I had not witnessed.

Finally, concerned in a very different way – in a way that carried a whiff of menace – she said, "I don't know who you think you are, or what you think you're doing, but stop it! You don't get to hear Dorothy's threats like I do. They're aimed at you, but I'm the one who has to hear them."

I closed my eyes. I could hear her words, of course, the warning that her rising tone and volume conveyed. I heard her say, "You have a job. You're good at it..."

I heard it all. But in the darkness behind my closed eyes, all I could see was Soul Man jumping to his death, choosing that over...

"She explicitly said you'll lose your job," Audrey almost shouted into the phone.

I suppressed an involuntary shudder, keeping my voice deliberately calm, matter-of-fact, but resolute. "I appreciate your telling me all this, Audrey, I really do. You're a friend. Just tell Dorothy I can't come in today."

Audrey tried one more pathetic "But..." I cut her off.

"Call you later."

That was the day before yesterday, days mostly spent at the San Francisco Public Library, where Grove and Hyde intersect at Market Street. The building is a relatively modern one, and it's peopled by the City's relatively modern population: among the usual denizens perusing call numbers as they seek a particular volume in the accessible stacks, or clutching the books they've found there, are the walking wounded of this great city.

The first floor reeks of the smell of the homeless, the unwashed doing their best in the large bathroom, some washing their clothes in the sinks, some their feet, and always a milling about. Outside, the mentally ill sit at long tables in front of computer screens talking to themselves, or to the phantoms they alone see, and even, occasionally, to other broken people occupying the same table.

I wandered from floor to floor, looking for a place to sit away from the stench, away from the madness. I found it on the 3rd Floor, barely more than a large alcove, but an alcove distinct and apart from the rest of the place. A plaque identified the space as the James C. Hormel Gay and Lesbian Center. There were books that explored their subjects – ancient Greece, religious writings of all kinds, history and resistance – through the lens of sexuality. Here, the marginalized gay community was celebrated both in books and in photos that adorn the dark wooden panels separating the shelves of books that nearly encircle the room. And here, too, was a quiet, dignified serenity.

As I settled in to read the pile of newspaper articles, magazine stories and books I had assembled from various floors of the library, I stopped wondering if the person at the next table, or those looking at books along the walls, were gay or not. I had found an oasis in the desert, a sanctuary where library conditions of my childhood still prevailed: reverence for the written word and a hushed respect for the place and the experience itself – almost like a temple.

The librarian in the periodical section of the A.V. Department, bored or stoned or both, agreed to retrieve a long list I'd given him of newspaper and magazine accounts of what occurred at Port Chicago on July 17, 1944. With almost every computer search I did, that date popped up, and I used it to assemble my list.

From the top of the stack now in front of me, I picked up some kind of official report, and began to read. I realized at once that my librarian assistant had thrown in something I hadn't asked for, a report of a more recent vintage. I don't know if this was just carelessness or something he thought I should know, but it certainly set the stage for Port Chicago, and that stage was a bloody one.

The report detailed a legal settlement between the U.S. Navy and five civilians concerning an event that had happened just twelve years before in 1987 – in my memory, but not remembered as the report detailed. The other patrons of this quiet library space must have thought that someone with Tourette's Syndrome had invaded their sanctuary because I kept shaking my head in disbelief, and sucking in my breath. To put it bluntly, the Secretary of the Navy in the Pentagon had decided that the best way to put a stop to a long-running protest at Port Chicago was to run a train over the protestors. Which is exactly what happened. The train, filled with weapons bound for Central

America, plowed into the well-publicized group of protesters, mostly Vietnam veterans, like the one who lost both of his legs when he fell under the train, which didn't stop until it was well past him. When I read that, I vowed to take a ride out to Port Chicago, so I could see for myself how this could have happened. And to see if I could feel the ghosts of those who died there 55 years ago when the ammunition they were loading from those trains into waiting ships blew them into smithereens.

I finished reading the report, convinced again by what I'd read that in so many respects, our government is indistinguishable from most others, protecting itself even if it has to maim or kill its own people. But even that reminder did not prepare me for what I was about to learn from the very next article I picked up from the stack.

The headline brought me instantly back to my reasons for being there, and reminded me that for Soul Man, it wasn't just jail and it wasn't maiming, it was non-existence. Under the banner of the San Francisco Examiner, dated July 19, 1944, the headline screamed in all CAPS: "322 KNOWN DEAD IN EXPLOSION: 500 INJURED."

The article left little for the imagination. "Only four bodies had been found," it reported, "and Navy officers said they expected to find few if any more. All others simply disintegrated in the vortex of an explosive force so tremendous that heavy steel deck plates turned white hot and shredded into shrapnel."

I read until closing time but still hadn't finished, so convinced my new best friend at the Periodical Desk on the floor below to keep my stacks – one read, one yet to read – on a shelf behind his desk. I had to promise on penalty of painful fines (even best friendship has its limits) to return the next day to retrieve them, as if I could have done otherwise.

My head was swimming. When I got home, the light on my answer machine summoned me; it would continue blinking until I answered the summons. Before I did that, though, I decided to fortify myself for what might be in waiting for me there. I took a pint of Dark & Hunky out of the freezer, and the carton of vanilla. While the chocolate turned soft enough to scoop, I fished a small pipe and some aromatic, green marijuana from under the fake bottom below the vanilla ice cream itself and broke off a piece of the herb to fill the bowl of the pipe. I served myself some ice cream, took two or three wonderfully satisfying spoonsful, savoring the cold smooth consistency, like edible silk made of dark chocolate, and then lit and inhaled two or three equally satisfying puffs on my pipe. I put the ice cream and the pot away, took a deep breath, and punched the playback button on the answer machine.

I sat through several versions of the same message from Audrey: "Call me!" Sometimes, the request had a "please" attached. Once, she attached another few words that would make me blush to write down. Between Audrey's entreaties, there was also a message from Dorothy. The words she appended to Audrey's basic message should have focused my attention like a hanging. "Call me at once!" I ignored the command.

My reward came in a long message at the end like dessert after my ice cream dinner. I heard the overlapping voices of two little girls who were head-over-heels in love with their new dog, and more than overjoyed to tell their Uncle Harrison every detail and every antic the answer-machine had time to record.

"Pee-Pee made Mama so mad," Ayusha giggled. "He ate one of Sasha's toys."

"He did not," Sasha interjected, cracking up with her sister, "he played with it." And on went the two laugh bugs to the end of the tape, for my repeated enjoyment.

I needed to hear those lovely children chortling like that. Their contagious laughter helped me regain some sense of equilibrium. What I'd read, not just about the traumatic force of that blast, but about what had happened to JJ – and not just to JJ, not even close – had unsettled me in a profound way. It was almost more than I could take in, and I would be taking in more the next day.

"I'll call them tomorrow," I said aloud, meaning Sasha and Ayusha. Still, I knew I also had to phone the two other callers. It's just that I wasn't thinking of them as I lay down to rest my eyes. When I woke, my heart was pounding. It was two in the morning. I tried to grasp at the remains of a dream. I had been sitting in front of a train that exploded. The force of the explosion must have blown me into the air, because I remember falling into the ocean. I think I tried to scream, but no sound came out.

Awake now, I started to process some of what I had learned. This was one of those American stories that we're ashamed to talk about, ashamed to acknowledge, another dark stain on our national character. But almost at the same moment I acknowledged this fact, a simultaneous thought: *Forget OUR shame. Acknowledge YOUR own!* And it was true. I had my own personal shame to bear for not knowing, for only now learning what we had done to these men because we could. And we could for one reason only: they were Black.

I undressed as I thought about how our history with race has poisoned our past, was still poisoning our present. And I thought of my own poisonous contributions. I thought about what Mr. Jeppards must have been thinking as he saw me lock my car door, and I wondered if that act of unconscious racism had provided him his last thought on earth.

Shivering, I lay down again, thinking about tomorrow's education, wondering if it would answer my questions about Soul Man, even as I feared the answers might torment my own soul.

# Chapter Thirteen

Ghosts. So many ghosts. I could not escape the eyes of the ghost of Soul Man that haunted me, and then I thought of the hundreds of eyes that must have haunted him, must have weighed him down – a weight he would carry with him into the dark waters of the San Francisco Bay.

I had left home early in the morning, in time to see the thick traffic congestion going in the opposite direction, west on Highway 24 at the height of rush hour into the metropolis – Oakland, Hayward, San Mateo, and, oh yeah, San Francisco. There were relatively few of us headed in the direction of Walnut Creek and Concord. And only one of us – me – heading toward the tiny village of Port Chicago.

It was hard to reconcile the tidy white houses with their manicured lawns and white picket fences with what I had read the day before. "The town of Port Chicago lay desolated, with not a single building intact." But then as now, the tiny town is dwarfed by the huge expanse of once idyllic countryside, now showing the results of its military rape: death-dealing weapons hidden under great pregnant mounds of grass-covered earth extending as far as one can see on one side; and, on the other side, a barren expanse leading down to Suisun Bay. Its waters, salted by Pacific Ocean currents passing under the Golden Gate Bridge into the Oakland Bay and through the Carquinez Straits, mix together with and are sweetened by snow-melted waters pouring down from the great Sierra Nevada Mountains that rise up in the East.

Like I said, I left early enough to see how lucky I was not to be in that bumper-to-bumper madness on the other side of the freeway, but not early enough to miss Dorothy's wake-up call. It came at 5:30 a.m., an unheard-of hour for Dorothy to be up and stirring. I wish I could say she woke me, but I had been up most of the night, reading the horror story that took place here 55 years earlier. At best, I had slept an hour or so, waking from dreams whose disturbing images I could never quite remember.

"This is Dorothy, and I hope I woke you up," she began, by way of greeting.

"Well, good morning to you, too." That was me, as chipper as I could be at that hour before sunrise.

The conversation continued. "Your selfishness – your obsession – is about to cost you your job," she almost hissed. "Do you know that?"

"Oh, come on, Dottie," a futile gesture to try to lighten things up on my part.

"Shut up!" on her part. "You think you're my biggest problem? You're not! It's my Board of Directors. They want your head." She waited.

"And?" I waited.

"You're accountable to me, and I'm accountable to them," she screamed. "Do you hear me?"

"Yes, I hear you, Dorothy," I said, getting all serious. "But right now, I can't be accountable to you. I'm sorry. I'm sorry what happened happened, but it happened. I can't unsee it. I wish I could. I'm sorry."

I felt, more than heard, the phone slam, and I figured that was the last time I'd be talking to Dorothy, and the last time I'd be seeing a paycheck for a while. I made a mental note to call my sister. She had bailed me out of more than one economic crisis over the years, and might have to again.

But I couldn't focus on any of that now; it had all happened before I stepped out of my car, before I saw the endless mounds of buried weaponry, including, I had no doubt, atomic bombs, like a deadly pox infecting the earth itself.

A rail track led from the main base gate, crossed the two-lane road, and continued through another gate on the other side down to the water. A Marine sentry standing as erect as a statue stepped in front of me as I tried walking through that gate.

"Private property, Sir," he said.

"Private? I thought this was a U.S. military base. Since when did they become private?"

"You can't go down there, Sir," he explained.

*****

I had read reports well into the night. What I read made me sick. Two ships and a train had been vaporized in the blasts that July, in 1944; 320 men had been killed, more than 200 of them Black. When the survivors – many still with visible injuries – were ordered to resume their mule-like duties, hand carrying boxes of ammunition onto waiting ships, most refused. Threatened with courts-martial for treason, a capital offense, most resumed their terrifying duties. Most, but not all. Fifty men, including JJ, were court- martialed. All the officers and all the members of the court were white. The 50 men facing a possible firing squad were Black.

Reading the transcripts of that court-martial through the night was excruciating:

*Question: "Seaman Second Class Dunn, on the 17th of July, did anything unusual happen?"*

*Answer: "Well, as soon as I got in bed, I was blown right back out."*

*Question: "How old are you?"*

*Answer: "Seventeen, Sir."*

*Question: "How much do you weigh?"*

*Answer: "104, Sir."*

*Question: "Did you know you could be shot for failing to obey an order?"*

*Answer: "Yes, Sir."*

*****

Question: "Lt. Tilban, do you know what happened to Seaman Second Class Dunn?"

Answer: "He had his arm in a sling."

Question: "On the morning of the 9$^{th}$ of August?"
Answer: "Yes, Sir."
Question: "Did he muster?"
Answer: "Yes, sir."
Question: "When he mustered he had his arm in a sling?"
Answer: "Yes, sir."
Question: "And you ordered him to go load ammunition?"
Answer: "That is right, sir."

*****

Question: "Seaman First Class McKinney, were you injured?"
Answer: "Yes, Sir. My bunk was smashed in on me."
Question: "Were you put in the hospital?"
Answer: "No, Sir, I wasn't. There were too many that were seriously injured to go to the hospital."

*****

Question: "Seaman Second Class Jeppards, were you injured?"
Answer: "Yes, Sir, I was. After the first blast, I fell down. By the time I got up, the second blast happened."
Question: "What injuries did you sustain?"
Answer: "I got a deep gash here in the joint on my right leg and my knee. They couldn't take all the glass out, and that's still aching. My right shoulder got hit with something heavy. I stayed in the hospital for more than a week."

*****

Seaman Second Class Jeppards. Joshua Jeppards. JJ. He and the others testified that the white officer overseers raced them against each other, betting on whose unit would work the fastest, rewarding the winners with statements like, "You're a credit to your race." Of course, that "compliment" was just one side of the coin. The other side of that coin is reflected in the sneering reprimand JJ was given when he refused to load more ammunition. "You're not only letting me down," his white overseer told him, "you're letting every Negro in America down. Take some pride in your race!"

It took the three-judge court just 80 minutes to convict all 50 men – just over one minute per defendant – and to sentence each to confinement for fifteen years, and a dishonorable discharge.

I thought of the horrifying mass shooting that had occurred earlier this year at a Colorado High School called Columbine, carried out not by terrorists, but by two armed high school students who killed a dozen of their fellow students and one teacher before taking their own lives. The mental images of that recent horror had now been superseded by new images of horror, one that had occurred more than 50 years before.

I tried to imagine what JJ and the others had survived, what they had witnessed and what they had endured since. It had taken more than three weeks for them to gather and sort body parts and debris. The great Supreme Court Justice Thurgood Marshall, who was then the sole attorney for the NAACP, represented the men in their appeal. In his closing argument, he asked, "What degree of confusion, terror and shock did each of these fifty men experience, seeing their friends piled up in baskets and pieces – an arm, a leg, or a head and a shoulder – picking up these remnants of human bodies?"

Appeal denied.

Consumed by the horror of it all – and suffocated with shame and guilt – JJ kept it all to himself for more than half a century. He had seen his friends blown to bits in front of him. He had sustained significant injuries. He had been court-martialed and imprisoned at

Fort Leavenworth, where fellow prisoners taunted him and the other "mutineers" for their "cowardice" and, of course, for their color. Any one of these events could drive a man insane, but taken together?

One man's suicide had driven me mad enough to risk giving up the best paying job I'd ever had, so how could that one man, how could Seaman Second Class Jeppards deal with the degree of trauma I was just beginning to understand? Now, I could understand a man committing suicide, unable to live under this crushing burden of memory. What I could not comprehend was why it had taken him 55 years to do it.

*****

I phoned Perry after a long, hot shower which did little to wash away the dirty reality of our shameful history. Lilla answered. I had forgotten that Perry had left that morning for the annual conference of the Black Police Officers Association in Atlanta. I gave her the two-bit description of my day, including my early morning confrontation with Dorothy.

"Come on over," she said. "The kids would love to see you. I'd love to see you. Even Pee-Pee would love to see you," she laughed.

Ah, laughter. How I needed to hear it.

"I'm really beat, Lilla. I don't think I'd be very good company."

"How 'bout breakfast tomorrow morning, then? Perry'll be calling in at seven. Wanna be here for that?"

"What's for breakfast?"

Another laugh. "See you in the morning."

# Chapter Fourteen

It was raining when I finally dragged myself out of bed. I had been tossing and turning for at least two hours, hoping to squeeze in just twenty more precious minutes of that ever-shrinking commodity: sleep. The cold, dark house matched my mood. I considered calling Lilla to beg off breakfast, but I knew the girls would be excited to tell me Pee-Pee stories, or show me his latest trick, and Lilla would be making me a real breakfast. Like me, the Datsun was barely able to start at all. It always took two or three times of turning the key and listening to the motor strain to start, before she coughed and sputtered to life. But now, that pattern seemed a thing of the past. I kept trying, mentally giving myself a limit of ten tries before giving up. She started, reluctantly, on the ninth attempt, so I just missed missing breakfast.

My gloom, a leftover from the day before, extended only as far as Lilla's front door. There's something about a small dog's excited barking, drowned out by a four-year-old's squeals of laughter, that puts you in the here and now.

The girls had time to show me Pee-Pee's latest trick (fetching a torn rag doll of a sheep or lion or hippopotamus, I couldn't tell which). They'd already had their breakfast. Lilla told me to get myself a cup of coffee while she put the final touches on her daughters' school and pre-school attire for the day: a blue woolen cap for Sasha, a long knitted scarf for Ayusha, identical whitish coats buttoned all the way up, and, finally, yellow rain slickers with attached hoods to keep the rain off.

The girls' carpool transportation arrived with a burst of horn honking, and Lilla, holding the hands of her children – so different from the horror visited on the children I knew from my work – escorted them down to the waiting car, which already held two other children. I watched them through the front window – watched as Lilla kissed each of them good-bye, and stood, without an umbrella, waving as the car slowly drove out of sight.

I grabbed a clean towel from the hallway linen closet where I knew Lilla kept them, and met her at the door. She took the towel and started drying her hair. "Thanks," she coughed.

"It's the least I could do for breakfast," I said, just as the phone started ringing.

"Full payment," she smiled, "requires that you answer that. Will you? It's gotta be Perry."

I did, and it was.

"Goddammit!" Perry said to my hello. "I'm not out of the house for two days before some man moves in on my wife!"

"I'm not some man," I protested, "I've been carrying on with your wife for years."

"I like an honest man," Perry said, and I could hear the twinkle in his voice. "So, what are you and my wife up to?"

"Having breakfast," I said. "Or, at least, I am. Having breakfast and licking my wounds."

"She wounded you?" he continued to joke. But the humor drained out of me, and the heaviness of the night and morning again descended, even with Pee-Pee jumping up and down around my legs, begging for attention.

"How's your conference going," I asked, not wanting to go where I knew the conversation was headed.

"Never mind," Perry replied, recognizing the shift in my voice, "it's just a conference. Anyway, it's over. I'm not even in Atlanta any more."

"Where are you?"

"I'll tell you after you fill me in. You've got something new. I can hear it."

I tried to give him a thumbnail sketch of what I'd read, what I'd seen, and what I'd felt, but there were no words I could find to do those feelings justice. And then, after a pause, I heard myself say something I had not planned for.

"Sorry, Perry. I feel like I'm carrying a heavy load on my back, and it hurts. It hurts. I'm not sure I can keep doing it."

"So, you're going be satisfied raising money for your ungrateful boss, and forget about JJ? I don't believe you." He didn't say it as a criticism, simply a matter-of-fact statement of his belief. He didn't believe I could forget about JJ. I didn't either, but there were consequences I hadn't considered.

"Oh, yeah," I added, as casually as I could. "I don't think I have a job anymore."

"What the hell have you done," Perry demanded.

"It's not what I've done; it's what I haven't done."

"Which is?"

"Well, to put it bluntly, go to work. I haven't gone into the office in the past few days. I tried to explain to Dorothy on the phone, and she hung up on me."

"You might want to spend the day trying to repair that relationship," Perry advised. "On the other hand, if you lose your job, you can always move in with Ayusha and Sasha. You and Pee-Pee can share a palette on the floor."

"Don't joke," I said. "It could come to that."

"Okay, I want to talk to my wife. But just know that you're not quitting. I'm not letting you quit. I'm hooked, and you hooked me. No fair jumping off it now."

"I really wish you wouldn't use that phrase, 'jumping off,'" I said. But what I really wished is that I could forget, and not just the jumping off. I wished I could forget about what Soul Man was never able to forget about. "He couldn't live with it," I said to Perry. "He couldn't bear the pain, and I understand that. It took him a long time, but..."

"But you're not there yet," Perry interrupted. "You're not even close. Now, let me talk to my wife."

"You were going to tell me what you found."

"Oh that. Well, you're not going to believe it."

There was a quality in his voice, an excitement that had the effect of bringing me back around. "I'm not going to believe what?" I was back in the marathon.

"JJ's prison records arrived at the Department, and they faxed them to me here."

"And?"

"And there was precious little information in them. Except for one very important bit." He had my full attention by now, and I tried to wait for whatever would follow his dramatic pause in the narrative, but couldn't contain myself.

"And? And?"

"And, guess what. He grew up in Rawlerson, Georgia. And guess where I am."

"Rawlerson, Georgia?"

"Exactly. It's only a couple of hours south of Atlanta."

"What do you think you're going to find there," I wondered aloud.

"Don't know 'til I find it," he replied, adding, "but I'm a damn good investigator. I'll bet you dollars to donuts that I have things to report by tomorrow."

"Aren't you coming home tomorrow? That's what Lilla told me."

"And, as always, she's right. I'll be taking the red-eye out of Atlanta. Gets into Oakland at some ungodly hour, like 6:35 in the morning. I'm planning on going straight to the gym to shave and shower. Meet me there at 8:00, and I'll fill you in."

"That's if you've got something to fill me in about."

"Oh, I'll have something, ye of little faith. Now, let me talk to my wife."

I said good-bye, and called for Lilla. She came from the kitchen wearing dry clothes. I could smell the bacon frying.

"There's a waffle in the iron on the counter," she said as she took the receiver from my hand. "If you want some eggs with that, make 'em yourself."

The tease of Perry's news had reignited the flame that I wanted to, but could not, extinguish. I wanted to think I'd solved the mystery of Soul Man's sudden departure from the earth, the traumas he had carried from Port Chicago that led to my trauma of witnessing his final act. But it was clear that Perry wasn't convinced, and the ball was now in his court.

I went into the kitchen just in time to see the waffle iron light go on. The bacon was crispy, like I like it, and the waffle was a perfect golden brown. Not only that, it came out of the iron without sticking. I poured myself another cup of coffee, slathered butter and honey on the waffle, nibbled at the bacon, and never once thought about ice cream.

How strange – no job, nothing to do now but wait, and yet I felt completely calm for the first time in days. I couldn't put the pieces together, but somehow, I felt they were falling into place.

I couldn't really hear Lilla's part of the conversation with Perry, but whatever they were saying to each other, her part was punctuated with loud bursts of laughter. Lilla's laughter was always uninhibited, always full-throated. And it always made me smile. If I was under the spell of an evil spirit cast on the Bridge, there were other spirits – animated by compassion and human decency, friendly spirits that served as counterweights.

The rest of the day would be spent waiting, something I'm very bad at. But, as I listened to Lilla's laughter, I lifted a forkful of waffle, dripping with honey, to my lips and savored it. The swirling emotions of yesterday that had threatened to disable me had passed. And so had the rain.

# Chapter Fifteen

I swear I could feel Soul Man's hands tight on my shoulders and shaking me. I looked down and saw skeletal digits, blanched bones that once were fingers gripping me.

"Wake up!" the specter screamed, and suddenly, I was awake, but the shaking didn't stop. The whole house shook, jolting me up and out of my bed, which continued to jump and jerk as I tried to gain a firm footing.

An earthquake at two in the morning! We Californians are used to such events, even when, as now, they arrived not in what we casually referred to as "earthquake weather" – hot, dry September days – but in cold, wet December days like today.

I had fallen asleep three or four hours earlier to the lullaby of rain on my roof, which calmed my roiling anticipation of hearing what Perry had learned. But now, I was wide awake. The rumble didn't last longer than five or ten seconds, though it easily seemed twice that long, but that was long enough to keep me from returning to sleep.

I turned the radio to the classical music station, which was playing the magnificent Schubert String Quintet with its lush harmonies and beautiful melodies seeming to soothe the whole house, and everything in it – except me. I consciously tried to put JJ out of my mind, letting the music carry me away. Of course, trying not to think of something – anything – only puts the thought squarely in mind. I gave the effort up entirely when the Schubert piece ended, and was followed by Beethoven's 7th, a beloved piece to be sure, but the very one that had been playing on my car radio when JJ went over the railing. Just as a scent wafting through the air can trigger a memory from childhood, I was back on the Bridge, shivering and afraid.

In my mind, I saw the cascading series of tragic events in Soul Man's life as great stones tethered to JJ by relentless memories, beginning with that catastrophic explosion in 1944, and ending in front of me more than fifty years later as I locked my car door in an act of self-protection. It was the weight of those stones, which pulled him to the bottom of the Bay, and the end of all memories.

I tried, again, to empty my mind. I watched a little mindless television, spooned up some mindless ice cream, and waited for dawn.

It still had not arrived when I set out in the dark just after 5:30 a.m. for the gym, not because I like going at that hour. I don't. The noise bouncing off the walls in the cavernous men's dressing room downstairs at that hour – mostly raucous recitations of yesterday's sports victories or losses – was like a steady assault on the ears (unless, of course, you were a sports fan, in which case I guess it was Beethoven to your ears.) The paper snowflakes and other decorative trappings of the season that adorned the walls did nothing to put me in the Christmas spirit.

Believe me, I hadn't planned to get here with the crowd trying to squeeze in a couple of hours of stationary cycling, or weight lifting, or track running, or any of a dozen other exercise regimens, before beginning their 9-to-5 jobs. It was the worst, the most crowded time to be here, but it was still better than being at home alone with the thoughts I could not escape.

This morning was no exception. Talk of the earthquake was on everybody's tongue – or, at least, the ubiquitous question, "Did you feel it?" Besides that, one could get a comprehensive glimpse of current events and Bay Area sports activities through the lens of the variety of cultures and people in this polyglot part of the country in the raucous laughter and wonderful patchwork of languages spoken here. Two older Chinese men competed to be heard in Cantonese; Spanish bounced around the room, from aisle to aisle, punctuated by loud Spanish curses – among the few words I understood. I recognized Vietnamese and Korean being spoken by small groups here and there, but could not identify all the languages or dialects I heard. Nor could I understand any of them, except for the universal language of laughter.

One very young African American man was warning a group of older men about what the media had dubbed "Y2K," a computer glitch that he was sure would bring chaos because computers had not been programmed for the imminent turn of the century. "Airplanes will fall out of the sky," he said, earnestly. "Society as we know it will end!" (I couldn't help but wonder if that would be such a bad thing.)

A rare Republican voice was disparaging President Clinton in particularly vulgar terms that began by denigrating the Senate for having cleared the President earlier in the year of articles of impeachment, and ended with a fiery, and very loud, denunciation of the President's very recent policy success on behalf of disabled people, allowing them to join the workforce without jeopardizing their Medicaid and Medicare coverage. "Might as well just give everyone free medicine," he grumped.

Perry would not get there for another two hours, so I showered before hitting the pool. I had learned to swim as a kid, my one and only concession to exercise. I always found the even, rhythmic strokes that carried me smoothly across the length of the pool and back to have a calming effect, quieting my racing mind. I did twenty laps before warming up in the steam room. It was better than waiting at home alone, where my thoughts haunted me even through the night.

I showered again, dressed quickly, and went upstairs to wait for Perry. True to its advertising promise, Southwest Airlines had arrived on time, and Perry got to the gym almost exactly at 8:00 a.m. He found me sitting outside under the cement overhang to avoid the drizzle and occasional spurt of rain, the end of a weak storm. He should have looked beaten from having just spent the night crammed into a seat with too little leg room. Instead, he looked as if he had just had the best night's sleep of his life. I was the one who looked beaten from lack of sleep, a cluttered mind, and my obsessive preoccupation with Soul Man.

We greeted each other with one of those man hugs, where neither of us knew quite how tightly to embrace the other, or quite where to put our arms. (Ah, the trials and tribulations of manhood in America!)

"How was the flight?" I asked.

"How are you planning to spend Christmas," he asked, by way of reply. I knew Perry well enough to know this was no casual question. *Where's he going with this?* I wondered.

"Christmas? I don't know," I said. "I haven't given it any thought Why?"

With one of his million-watt smiles animating his face, he said, "You should start practicing your Mele Kalikimakas." And with that bit of instruction, he turned to enter the building, looking back long enough to say, "Wait for me here."

I could have strangled him! It was a classic Perry tease – dropping a tantalizing clue about something he knew, and something he knew I wanted to know.

I clucked my tongue at Perry's retreating back, and followed him into the building, but not down the stairs. I grabbed a paper cup of cold water, and sat at a counter up against a huge plate-glass window that looked down onto the pool. Someone had left the morning paper, and I scanned the headlines, none of which drew me to read the accompanying articles. I watched the swimmers below, some with the sleek muscled bodies of athletes powering their way back and forth across the length of the pool. But most looked more like the Pillsbury Dough Boy in shades ranging from pasty pinkish-white to glistening bluish-black – and splashing clumsily together in the large group section roped off from the four double-wide discreet lanes separated by long blue and white lengths of plastic.

One of the larger of the human whales was a short, off-white racial blend of a man whose non-stop mantra I was very familiar with, as was everyone else who had ever shared the dressing room with him. "Easy! Gentle! Easy! Gentle!" he'd say, but loud enough to disrupt any possibility of ease or gentility. Even now, though he was a full floor below me and separated by thick glass, I could still hear him. "Easy! Gentle!" he said, as he slowly lowered himself into the pool under a banner strung across the ceiling proclaiming "Peace on Earth."

But the truth is, I was just killing time, nothing more. "Mele Kalikimaka," Perry had teased. I watched the second hand sweep around the old-fashioned clock on the wall behind the sign-in desk, which seemed to slow down in direct proportion to my ever-increasing anxious anticipation.

Mele Kalikimaka. Merry Christmas. Our mother had taken my sister and me to Honolulu one Christmas when we were in elementary school, and we'd all become quite fluent in Mele Kalikimaka. The words had become a running joke between the two of them. My sister would say to my mother, "Don't touch Harry. He's suffering from a bad case of mele kalikimaka!" To which my mother might respond, "Oh? I thought that's what we ate at last night's luau."

I was too young to understand the humor of their repartee, so I'd say, in leaden literalness, "You're both wrong. It means Merry Christmas." And they'd roll their eyes and laugh.

I waited there for about twenty minutes before deciding to go downstairs, where I found Perry in the last row of lockers. He was standing on wet towels, and getting dressed. When he saw me, he wagged an accusing finger. "I told you to wait for me," he scolded.

"Which you knew I could not and would not do for long. The suspense is killing me. What did you mean, Mele Kalikmaka?"

"I meant Merry Christmas, of course," he said, his eyes twinkling like Santa Claus.

"Perry!"

"Okay, okay," he said. "Don't have a stroke."

"Then tell me what you found," I pressed.

"Plenty," he said.

And, for the next twenty-five minutes, I sat in stunned silence, in awe of Perry's skills as an investigator.

Describing Rawlerson as a "bum-fuck racist backwater of a town," he said there were no Jeppards in the phone book, so he went to the local high school in search of old year books in which JJ might have made an appearance, perhaps leaving clues to follow. He had asked the school librarian where yearbooks from the early 1940s might be found, and she had replied, "White or colored?'

The high school – named for Robert E. Lee – had integrated after a prolonged struggle defined by multiple court orders and multiple defiance of court orders. "The colored year books," the librarian had explained to Perry, "are in boxes in the janitor's storeroom."

She had called the janitor on the school intercom, and he arrived in the office a few minutes later, a stooped Black man who escorted Perry to a poorly constructed shed filled with garden tools, cleaning supplies, and stacks of yellowing paper and boxes of yearbooks with dates handwritten on the outside.

"Can I see those yearbooks from 1940 to 1943," Perry had asked.

"Yes, Sir," the old man had replied, adding, "I'm prob'ly in one of them books." The old man had gotten through the tenth grade, he explained, back in 1941, before joining the Army.

"You were a student here in 1941," Perry had pressed.

The old man chuckled. "Well, it weren't here, exactly," he said. "We had our own school down the road apiece. It ain't there no more." He asked Perry what he was looking for.

And Perry told him. "I'm looking for someone who might have been a classmate of yours. Joshua Jeppards. You know him?"

"Not him," the old man had answered. "But I knowed his little sister, Letty."

Perry asked him if he was sure it was Joshua's sister, to which the janitor replied, "Course I'm sure. We even sparked a couple times." Perry said the old man had laughed at the memory, revealing the three or four teeth still left in his mouth. Then he added, somewhat unnecessarily, that Letty's little brother had got himself into a lot of trouble back in the war. "He done went to prison," he said, shaking his head.

"And what happened to Letty," Perry asked, with growing excitement.

"Oh, she passed a few years back," he had answered, with some delicious details, which Perry related verbatim, mimicking the old man's drawl. "She had some kids. Got a daughter live just a couple mile from here. She gettin' up in age, a widow, but she spry enough, I reckon."

"Her name?" Perry had asked, trying not to sound too eager.

"Can't rightly recall." Perry thought he might have run into a wall, until the old man added, "But I can take you to her house."

I don't think Perry could possibly have been as excited at that moment as I was now. I sat there, shaking my head in disbelief, my mouth agape, completely oblivious to the echoing din of the locker room.

Perry offered to drive the janitor home in exchange for showing him where Letty's daughter lived. The old man directed him to a house in a tidy part of town, with neat rows of well cared-for houses, one of which he identified as hers. Then Perry drove him home, describing the experience as "going from the paved part of town to the Old South, with unpaved dirt roads right out of *To Kill a Mockingbird*."

"Just tell me what you learned," I said, loud enough to silence the two men dressing nearby, bantering in animated Spanish. They looked as if they expected me to throw a punch, and I couldn't tell if they hoped it wouldn't come to that – or, that it would.

"Sorry," I said to them. "*Lo siento.*" I turned back to Perry, imploring him with my eyes.

"Okay. Okay," he said in a low voice designed to calm me down. He had been taken aback, he said, by how middle class the house looked where Letty's daughter lived, how well manicured the front lawn was with its perfect purple fuchsia border. "I guess I was expecting that every Black person there lived in poverty. Does that make me a racist?" Perry asked with a grin.

"Probably," I answered, without one.

"Now here comes the good part," he continued. "A woman opened the door, maybe 60, but with that erect bearing of a soldier. I told her I was looking for a relative of hers, and asked if she could help me. If I weren't a Black man, she might have closed the door in my face, but she invited me in. She invited me in, but that was it. She never sat down, and neither did I. We stood and talked in a very clean living room, dotted with furniture kept pristine under clear plastic: a couple of sofas against adjoining walls facing overstuffed chairs arranged between flowering poinsettias against the opposite walls. A beautifully decorated Christmas tree was in the middle of the room, and smelled deliciously of pine. I don't know how many people live there, but there must have been two dozen presents, all wrapped in reds and greens, under the tree waiting to be opened," Perry said, as if that were the end of the story.

This time, the urgency in my voice came out in a menacing whisper. "Perry!"

"Here's the thing," he said. "The walls were covered with framed photos of Black men and a few women, all in military uniform. Oh, there were a few family portraits among them, but only a few."

"Meaning?" I urged him on.

"Meaning she comes from a military family."

"I don't care about that," I said, my impatience again getting the better of me. "I want to know what she told you."

"Well, a good investigator would care about that, 'cause when I asked her about Mr. Jeppards, she stiffened even more. Pursing her lips, she said, 'All the men in my family going back to the Civil War have been decorated military men, mostly officers. All but one, that is.'"

"Soul Man?" I asked Perry.

"Exactly," he said. "Soul Man. Which is not how she described him."

"Which was…?"

"Which was traitor," Perry answered.

"Traitor! What did she say, exactly?"

"She said only one member of the family ever brought 'shame and dishonor. That man!' She said it like she was spitting. And when I asked her who I could talk to about him, she was adamant. 'No one,' she said, firmly. 'No one has talked to that man in years, and no one will talk to you, either.'"

There had to be more, otherwise why the Mele Kalikimaka remark? "Was that it?" I asked, knowing it wasn't.

"Not quite," Perry said with a grin. "I tried an old trick. I pulled out my police ID and flashed my badge. In my most official voice, I told her, 'This is a police matter, Ma'am. Now, who can I talk to?' Her eyes got real big when she saw my badge, and she drew herself up even straighter. And then, pay dirt!"

"Only one ever talked to him, s'far as I know, is Pearley, and that talk did not go well, the way I heard it."

Here it was. A real name. A real person. I held my breath as Perry finished the story, pressing her for details.

"Pearley? How can I find her? Pearley who? But she was through talking."

"I already told you more than I should've," she told Perry. "I'm not sayin' any more. And Pearley ain't gonna talk to you, either."

"If you know, you must tell me where she lives," Perry pressed, adding, "It's a crime to lie to a law enforcement officer."

"She's in uniform in Hawaii somewhere. I don't even know where, and I wouldn't tell you if I did."

Perry tried one last time, asking "What's Pearley's last name?" At that point, she told him to get out of her house, which he did.

I was struck dumb, but Perry filled the silence. "Which is why I envy you," he said. "I got a trip to bum-fuck racist Rawlerson, and you get a trip to Honolulu. Mele Kalikimaka!"

So, here was another huge boulder pulling Soul Man down, down, down. Another huge layer of scorn had been heaped on him, a weight I hadn't considered: his own people turning on him. Patriots! Veterans! Good Americans who could not abide their boy's failure to follow orders. What thoughts must have gone through JJ's head as he tried to make sense of the world he knew best as he saw it falling apart?

Perry interrupted my wandering thoughts with a practical question. "So, when do you think you'll be leaving?"

"But we don't even know who we're looking for," I protested, even as my mind was pondering how to get there.

"Weren't you listening," Perry chided. "We know she's in the military. We know she's in Hawaii. We know she's almost certainly an officer. We know her name is Pearley. And, judging from the majority of those framed photos, she's probably in the Navy. That's a helluva lot of information for any investigator to follow."

"But..."

"And one more thing," Perry added, cutting me off. "We know that ex-wives and ex-girlfriends know where all the bodies are buried, and are always willing to talk about them. My favorite witnesses."

"But it's like looking for a needle in a haystack," I said, still stunned by this tide of new information.

"More like looking for a needle in a pin cushion," Perry said.

"But I have a job," I protested.

"Had a job," Perry reminded me. "But have a sister, as I recall, with money to burn. When was the last time you saw her? I'll bet she'd love to vacation with her little brother in Waikiki...`"

# Chapter Sixteen

I phoned Renni, but she wasn't home. You never knew about my sister. She did as she pleased, and she could just as well be or not be at home at any particular hour of the day. She might be back the next moment, or the next month.

Which meant that MY next moment would be spent making a call I wished I didn't have to make, but knew I did. I needed to know my status at F.A.C.T. – if, in fact, I had any status at all. This was the time where all the final details of "The Fundraiser" – as the president of the board always referred to it – would have kept me from sleeping, even after working 16-hour days. I wasn't sleeping, all right, but it had nothing to do with "The Fundraiser." What had obsessed me in my job had now been replaced by a new obsession entirely. What I could not get out of my thick skull was the picture of Soul Man, and then no man. No man.

Or, maybe, it was that this "No Man" had become all too real. The picture was too close for comfort, too close to put out of my mind. The man who had no existence for me at all while he lived, now occupied virtually all my thoughts day and night. And yet, only in death had he come alive.

Yes, I was curious about how the office was handling the last details of the annual fundraising Dinner, but I'm slightly embarrassed to acknowledge that it was a passing curiosity. Apparently, my mind was too small to entertain both obsessions at the same time.

Audrey answered on the third ring.

"Good morning. We are 'Fostering Abused Children Together'," she chirped, "Audrey speaking. How can I help you?" I didn't miss much about the office, but I did miss that voice.

I returned her greeting. "Morning, Beautiful," I said.

"Harry! Where have you been? I've never seen Dorothy as furious about anything as she is about your..." She paused, trying to find the right word to describe my behavior.

"My what?" I prompted.

"I don't even know what to call it."

"Just tell me if I'm still employed," I pressed.

"Does it matter? Looks like you don't care, one way or the other," she said, trying her best to sound like Dorothy, and failing. She just could not keep her natural upbeat personality from inflecting everything she said. Without the genuine menace that would have been part of the same sentiment coming out of Dorothy's mouth, Audrey's reprimand only made me smile.

"I care about you, my dear. How are you, Audrey?"

"I'm pissed," she said, sounding pissed. "I'm doing your work and mine. At least what was your work."

"Was?"

"You're fired," she said, sounding more astonished than I at the revelation. "She fired you. I tried to defend you, but I couldn't. That Cabrillo woman, she's something else. What's the opposite of subtle?" Audrey had a way of interrupting herself with a stray question, the way others might say "er" or "uh," buying time to think of what to say. She waited for an answer.

"Direct?" I suggested.

"Yes, direct," she said. "She made a direct threat. Not subtle! If Dorothy didn't let you go, they'd've let her go!"

"How do you know that," I asked.

"I was listening in on the call," she giggled. And I knew she was telling the truth. Audrey often listened in on Dorothy's calls, keeping me ahead of the curve. Because of this "little habit" as Audrey called it – and her affinity for me – I always knew what the Board of Directors or the Executive Director would be asking me to do well ahead of actually being asked. As far as I was concerned, Audrey was one of the perks of this job.

"What about the Dinner?" I asked her, unexpectedly.

"What about it? It's happening. Is that direct enough? What else do you need to know?"

"You're mad, aren't you?"

"No, I'm not. You are. You're mad as... Who's that rabbit in Alice in Wonderland?"

"The one she followed down the hole? The one who kept saying, 'I'm late. I'm late. I'm late?'"

"You know what I mean, Harry. Don't tease me. I'm talking about the other rabbit. The one at the tea party."

"Ah, the March Hare," I said.

"No. Not the rabbit. I mean the other guy at the tea party." Again, Audrey waited for an answer.

"Let me see," I teased. "Are you talking about the Mad Hatter?"

"Yes," she squealed. "You're mad like the Mad Hatter."

"You mean 'as mad as'," I couldn't resist saying.

"Why are you doing this, Harry?" There was such sincerity in that question, it made me embarrassed for covering up real emotions with my lame stand-up routine.

I had given a lot of thought to the very question Audrey had asked. Why was I doing this?

"I don't think I can answer that question," I told her. "Anyway, I know I can't answer it in any way that makes sense. Even if I understood why; even if I could tell you why; even if I could open my brain or my heart or my something and show you what's inside, you'd still be left with the same question."

This time I waited for Audrey to say something. But she said nothing, so I continued.

"I don't know why I'm doing it, Audrey. All I know is that I can't not do it."

For a moment, both of us remained silent. And then, there she was, chirping away like normal. Something I said, as clumsy as it was, had found a place to settle in her.

"Then can you help me write the ad?" she asked.

I wish I knew what it was I had said that let her shed her anger so easily. She seemed to understand something that I was still struggling to understand. How could it be that, somehow, I had given her the key to accept whatever it was I was doing, but could not find the lock in myself to use it on?

"The ad for what?" I asked.

As bright as a meadowlark, she chirped, "Your job."

I laughed out loud. Ah, Audrey. How lucky they are to have you there. That thought led to another, and this one carried a little pain: how lucky I have been to have had you there.

"I'll tell you what, Audrey, dear. Let's do it together. How about... are you writing this down?"

"Okay, go ahead."

So I did. I dictated the entire ad while Audrey took it all down.

*****

I tried Renni again, and again got no answer, which kindled a memory of an earlier failure to answer, or, at least, a refusal to do so. My sister wasn't always Renni. Her name used to be Rinni, but she didn't like that, so she changed it. Actually, it used to be Irene, if you want to get technical about it. I mean, that's the name our beloved mother gave her, Irene Breckenridge Shakovitz. My savior of a sister did something about that by the time she was eight years old. I was there when it happened.

Even though I was two years younger, we shared an elementary school classroom. It was a two-room schoolhouse with grades 1 through 3 in one room and 4 through 6 in the other. When Mrs.

Wilson called the roll on the first day of my first grade, Irene, then in the third grade, remained silent when her name was called. Mrs. Wilson – who had been her first and second grade teacher, and would be my second and third grade teacher – had known my sister as Irene for two years already.

"Irene," Mrs. Wilson said the second time, looking directly at my sister, who remained mute. And then, "Irene!" she almost barked, a far cry from the tone she usually used for children and adults alike, as if every utterance should begin with a bright, "Now, boys and girls..." The sharpness in her voice seemed to get everyone's attention except for my sister, who looked up, sweet as can be, and asked, "Oh, are you talking to me?"

Mrs. Wilson, that tower of tolerance – a part of every successful elementary school teacher's arsenal – scowled at my sister, as I sat among the first graders wishing that Irene had waited just one more year to declare her independence. That way, she'd be in the classroom next door, and I wouldn't be feeling like disappearing through a hole in the floor.

"Yes, little girl!" Mrs. Wilson almost hissed. "I AM talking to you!" I swear I heard a pin drop.

"My name's Rinni," my sister said, still sweetly, but with an edge that for anyone who knew her, which was everyone in the room, served as a warning, like the rattlesnake on the Gadsden Flag ("Don't tread on me!"). Only the foolish would ignore that warning, and even they would have trod carefully.

"Rinni?" demanded an incredulous Mrs. Wilson.

"Here," my sister answered. And that was the end of it. She was Rinni until she decided to become Renni, and she's been Renni as long as most people can remember. Not me, though. I remember everything, including the fact that my eight-year-old sister's act of self-assertion gave me the courage to do the same thing, even if it took me more than a decade, and the milestone of high school graduation to find it.

After high school graduation, Renni had gone on to get an advanced degree from Oberlin College in animal husbandry, and had become wealthy enough to qualify as rich, but through a different kind of husbandry. She made her money the old-fashioned way; she married it. By the time she was thirty-seven, she had acquired and discarded three husbands, each richer than the last. Or, as she liked to say, "I traded up."

She had started in the same humdrum way most young people do, marrying the teenage "love of her life" – a Latino hippie named Josue Ortega who soon inherited a fortune from a Colombian drug dealing uncle he did not even know he had. That gave him the wherewithal to pursue his life-long dream of becoming a ski bum. Unfortunately for him, Renni did not share that life-long dream, so, soon after he moved them to Aspen, she divorced him, using her share of his fortune to move to the desert outside Taos, New Mexico. Her nearest neighbors were more than a mile away, and she liked it that way. When, during her first winter there, she learned it was a snowbird's haven, she chose those times to vacation in warmer climes, like Costa Rica, Rio de Janeiro and Kuala Lumpur. I started calling her Snow Bunny, because she would do anything to avoid the cold, and she started calling me Shorty. I was 6'2".

She liked her second husband more than I did. He was a banker whom I insisted on calling by his first name, because he hated it: Cosmo! I can't even remember his last name, but I remember when she divorced him, and more than doubled her fortune.

My favorite was her third and, so far, last husband, Laurence Shotwell Cummings, some kind of software genius who created a program for making blueprints that some huge construction conglomerate paid him nearly a billion dollars for. Laurence with a "u" not a "w." I drove him crazy by calling him Larry. She got rid of him because he couldn't tolerate being called Larry.

Renni never really loved any of them, though she thought she loved the hippie. Her casual relationship with marriage (and her less than casual relationship with money) was one of the things I loved about my sister. She decided early on that if she was going to defy the odds regarding the financial status of post-divorced women, she would be the best odds defier ever. Yeah, I loved that about her.

We didn't talk on the phone much, but whenever we did, we fell into a comfortable rhythm. It was like we were just picking up a conversation we hadn't finished the day before. It was a rhythm we both knew well.

I dialed her number again, picturing her now in her shorts and halter, ready to go riding off into the desert sunset, or just lolling on a rock, lizard-like, next to her backyard pool, which she kept heated even when the New Mexico temperature roared into the triple digits. And then it dawned on me that ski bums were now arriving in Taos in droves, not a good time to reach my heat-seeking missile of a sister. So I was doubly surprised when she answered – both because she was there, and because of how she answered the phone.

"Aloha," she said brightly, on the first ring.

"Aloha? What kind of shid is that," I asked. "Most people just say hello." The coincidence or kismet or whatever you want to call it wasn't lost on me. I just had no interest in pursuing whatever cosmic significance her greeting might portend.

"Shorty!" she screamed. "Shit! Shit! Shit! You little fart, where the fuck are you?"

"Don't curse like that, little sister, or Mom'll wash your mouth out with soap!"

"I thought you were someone else," she said. "I'm waiting for someone special to call. That's who I thought you were."

"Sorry to disappoint you," I said. "Who is he, the head of the Honolulu Chamber of Commerce?"

"Chamber of Commerce," she said derisively. "Small potatoes! As it happens, he owns a fleet of yachts that ply the waters off the entire Hawaiian Island chain. You can't imagine how amazingly in demand they are by the rich and bored of the world. Of course, a man of your poor breeding could never understand such things."

"Didn't we have the same breeding, you and I?"

"Yes," she agreed, "but some of us have overcome that limitation and some of us have not..."

"Are you getting married again?"

Renni laughed like no one else you've ever heard. It was loud and it was big, but it was also inviting. It brought you in, made you want to laugh along with her. I always felt, despite the swelling power of it, that she was really holding something back, like there was some delicious secret just beyond that expansive outburst, like if she were alone in the woods and heard something funny, the reverberation of her laugh would rival the proverbial tree falling in the forest.

"No, I'm not getting married," she said, taming her laughter. "Are you?" She laughed again.

"No, Sis, but I do need your help."

Renni was instantly serious. We knew each other well. She waited, knowing I needed no prodding.

"Some things have happened in the last few days that have left me unsettled. And in the last few hours, I've learned that I need to go to Honolulu to see if I can settle them."

"Unbelievable!" she shouted. "It's fate! I know it is! My horoscope said something wonderful would be happening soon in my life, and here it is."

"How do you know it's not your yachtsman that's supposed to be that wonderful happening?"

"Oh, him," she said, forgetting how much he seemed to have meant to her just a moment before. "I'm wiring you a ticket right now! Hold on... There's one leaving Oakland at 3:30 in the afternoon. Can you leave tomorrow?"

It was real now. I had no time to think. My own horoscope had promised no such "something wonderful," but Renni's had, and I was it.

"Tomorrow? Yeah, I guess so. What'll I do when I get there?"

"I have a house. Didn't I tell you? I can't believe I didn't tell you."

I could believe it. Easily. I hadn't learned that she'd left Josue in the snow until months after she established herself in Taos.

"It's right on the water at Blue Point. Damn!" she said, an astonishingly well-deserved interjection. "I bought it, oh I don't know, maybe nine or ten months ago." She said it as an afterthought. "You can have the whole bottom floor to yourself. It has its own entrance, its own kitchen and bathroom. It's just sitting there. No one uses it. We never even go down there. It's like two houses in one."

I had long since stopped being surprised by the choices my sister's upwardly mobile lifestyle allowed her to make. So, the fact that she had another house in the sun didn't surprise me. The fact that it was where I needed to be did.

"And I'll be there," she added. "I just got my own ticket while you were thinking of what to say. You're leaving in the afternoon on Aloha Flight Number 303. But guess what. I'm leaving tonight. I get to be there to meet you at the airport. It's gonna be so much fun. You're gonna love Kiki."

Kiki! "I don't think so, actually," I said, "but Honey, this is not a vacation thing. I can't explain what's going on over the phone, but this is something different. And it involves Hawaii. Maybe. To be honest, I'm not altogether sure, but I... I just have to find out. I have to know. I may even get my annual Christmas bonus, so I can pay you back..."

"Oh, shut up," she ordered. "If you can't spend it, why marry?" She was howling again, and I couldn't help but feel an old twinge, one that I had felt numerous times in our history together. One day, it would be me in a position to help her. That would be nice, anyway. But that day wasn't today, and we both knew it. Renni had climbed to the top of America's "classless society," and I was about to be the beneficiary of her success.

My sister had always been as daring, as willing to step into the unknown, as I was cautious, always wanting to know where to put my feet before leaping. Always until now, that is.

I was on my way to Hawaii. Although it was Christmastime, it was not sugar plum fairies that danced in my head, but sugar cones with a rainbow of brand-new ice cream flavors. And something else, too.

"Thank you, Renni," I said feebly, aware of how inadequate it sounded, but knowing there were no words adequate to express what I really felt.

"Shut up," she said again. "I'll see you tomorrow. I can hardly wait."

# Chapter Seventeen

I sat, squeezed between a teenager in the window seat and an older woman whose friends would have described, charitably, as "full-bodied." She was fat. I knew, by the time we landed in Honolulu five hours later, she would hate me. Not only would I jump visibly each time the plane hit even the slightest bump, I would have to get up and go to the bathroom three or four times. Nerves were responsible for most of those bathroom visits, but the three cups of coffee I'd had before boarding, one at home and two at the airport, might share some of the responsibility.

I am the world's worst air traveler, even when I have an aisle seat and can move around at will. My hands start to sweat even before I board, and they remain wet well into the flight, at least until the pilot has turned off the "Fasten Seat Belt" sign. In a futile effort to tame my fear, I'd developed my own strategy: stare at my sweating palms derisively as the plane struggles to escape inertia, and gains speed as it rumbles down the taxiway on its way to liftoff. (*Oh, please let us lift off!*)

The teen in the window seat was plugged into some kind of device that made him oblivious to everything other than the music that kept his head bobbing up and down, though he did smile once in my direction as the fat lady grunted when I asked her, for the fourth time, to let me back into my middle spot. She ordered three red wines, one after another, while she ate a non-stop "meal" of M&Ms, sugar cookies, and a variety of other snacks she'd carefully packed in her carry-on luggage. Mercifully, she said not a word to me until the very end, though the nasty expression on her face each time I had to ask her to let me out, and then back in, made it clear that she had things to say that I was glad she didn't. Only when the pilot announced that we had begun our descent, the signal for me to start staring again at my wet palms, did she turn toward me and snort, "Oh, my goodness. Get over it!"

I was on my way, but in truth, I was flying blind. If only I had instruments I could rely on like the ones that lifted this gigantic bird off the runway and kept it aloft until they guided the machine to a safe landing. (More praying.) The only thing I knew for sure was that I was looking for a woman named Pearley, though not one named Jeppards. Perry had already exploited his military contacts, and ascertained there was no active-duty officer with that last name on any of the many military bases that dot the Islands. As the plane prepared to land, my fear was mixed with excitement about seeing my sister, and real doubt about how I might go about the task Perry had said I was there to do. Finding Pearley seemed only a distant possibility, and if I did find her, what would I ask her? "Ex-wives and girlfriends know where all the bodies are buried," Perry had said, but whose bodies was I asking her about? I just didn't know.

The plane touched down and roared down the taxiway, ironically, my favorite part of the flight. Though I'd been told numerous times to follow the warning to "keep your seatbelts fastened until the plane comes to a complete stop at the gate," I always celebrated being back on *terra firma* by immediately unbuckling the belt as we sped down the runway, thrilling to the powerful engines as it felt like they were being throttled back.

There were no grass-skirt-clad *wahines* (as I had learned was the Hawaiian word for woman by reading the in-flight magazine) to hand out flower leis, and I walked quickly through the terminal to baggage claim, a series of carousels outside the building in the open air of Honolulu. The warm air itself felt perfect, cooled by a tropical breeze perfumed by ginger blossoms, plumeria flowers, and a vague scent of vanilla. I had left the mostly black and white world of Oakland and stepped into a world peopled by bronze-skinned beauties with bright hibiscus flowers in their hair, some blood red, some fiery orange, some a beautiful yellow. Discounting my nearly forgotten childhood excursion, if someone could fall in love with a place at first sight (or first smell), it happened to me there in baggage claim.

Renni was there without Kiki. She put a thick lei of purple and white flowers around my neck. We embraced briefly, looked each other up and down, and pronounced ourselves satisfied. She was wearing a loose-fitting green and black Hawaiian muumuu, open-toed sandals that showed off her toe nails, painted green and black to match her muumuu, and smelled sweetly of the plumeria blossom lei around her neck.

"Shorty," she repeated loudly and often. I'm sure the other passengers waiting for their bags to come tumbling down the chute onto the conveyor belt wished for my bag to come soon so we would exit out of earshot. But it was not to be; we were among the last standing there waiting.

"So, the Snow Bird has landed in Paradise," I said.

"You have no idea. It's the most beautiful place on earth," she gushed. "You're gonna love it here." I didn't dispute the prediction, but didn't think I'd be there long enough to appreciate all that she wanted to show me.

"What are you doing here?" she asked. I wasn't able to complete even the first sentence of the answer to that question before a voice two carousels away boomed, "Harry Ass! Harry Ass Shakovitz!"

It had been more than thirty years since I had been subjected to and demeaned by the junior high school bullies that found that label so funny. But all those years did not protect me from the involuntary reaction of my body: I trembled; my stomach tightened. I was a 7$^{\text{th}}$ grader again, afraid and small. I saw the man who had yelled walking quickly toward us, a broad smile on his face, as I looked for a way to escape. And though that face was older, I recognized it as my principal tormentor, the bully of bullies. I couldn't remember his last name, but his first name jumped immediately into my mind: Butch! (Or was that just what we, who had been his daily victims, called him?) He was in the 8^th grade when he found me to pick on, and much taller than I was then, but now he seemed so much smaller than I remembered him. And there was that smile.

As he reached us, he put his hand out for me to shake, but that gesture was met by a blast from Renni, who pushed his hand away.

"Who the hell do you think you are, you prick," she said, in her usual subtle way. I noticed the few people who were still waiting for their luggage step back, giving us space.

"Renni!"

But once launched, she couldn't pull herself back. "There is no one here named Harry," she said, "and the only hairy ass is yours, you fucking piece of shit."

The smile on his face dissolved into a mask of embarrassed distress.

"Renni!" I said again, louder than before.

"I... I..." Butch stuttered, trying to say something, but Renni cut him off.

"Look, Buddy, I don't know who you are, but let me introduce you to me and my little brother here."

*Oh, brother*, I thought, *here we go.*

"I'm Renni Breckenridge Shakovitz Ortega Moreau Cummings," she said, in her haughtiest voice. *Oh yeah,* I remembered, *husband number two's last name was Moreau.* Besides having kept their money, Renni's serial marriages allowed her to keep all their names, a list she trotted out whenever, like now, she thought it sounded most impressive, like a title of nobility. "And this is Harrison Q. Ovitz," she continued. "Do not disrespect him again." She threw that middle initial in because she thought the Q. gave me gravitas. "Now, who the fuck are you?" she demanded. So much for gravitas.

"I knew your brother in junior and senior high," he said, as meek as a mouse. This was certainly not the Butch I remembered. He looked genuinely scared. "My name is Ted. Ted Paulson."

"I always thought your name was Butch," I said as calmly as I could, trying to bring my sister down to earth. Something in Butch's demeanor released the knots in my stomach, let me relax my tightened shoulders.

He turned from Renni to me. "Yeah. I know. Butch was how I acted then. Your sister is exactly right. I was a fucking piece of shit." With that, he reached into his breast pocket and pulled out a business card, and handed it to me. Without looking at it, I stuffed it into my pants pocket. "I am so, so sorry," he said, then turned and walked out of the terminal.

I didn't know what to say, but Renni had no problem. "What an asshole," she said to his retreating back. "How do you know him?"

"7th grade," I said. "He was my bully in chief. He made my life miserable in middle school. I wasn't the only one he picked on, but I was probably the smallest, which made me the easiest target. I hated him."

"Now I do, too," she said, pulling me into her embrace. "You're with me now, so you're safe." And, I felt safe. To be completely honest, though, I always felt safe waiting for my luggage to arrive after a flight. It was the touchdown and disembarking that made me feel safe, far more than my sister's well-intentioned hug.

Renni kept up a steady stream of commentary as she drove me in a green Jeep from the airport, at first on a busy freeway, but soon through the heart of things along crowded Kalakaua Avenue, Waikiki's main thoroughfare. The International Marketplace was on my left, and a string of high-rise hotels stretched along the beach on my right. Dusk was descending, but I could see dark-skinned surf boarders and windsurfers crisscrossing each other's watery paths well beyond where much whiter tourists played in the surf breaking on the shore.

"That's the Royal Hawaiian Hotel," she said, pointing to a grand and beautiful old hotel, perhaps six stories high, no more, and painted a distinct flamingo pink. "We're going to have dinner there after we unload."

It was about ten more minutes, following the coast around the base of Diamond Head Crater before we turned down a small road leading off to the right toward the sea. The last fifty yards, or so, were unpaved, which didn't slow Renni up at all, and we bounced in ways that would have scared me to death in the air, before pulling up next to what looked like a Porsche, though I couldn't be sure of that. The huge house, lit with subdued outside light, was beautiful, all glass on top, all paneled below. A handsome bronzed man, considerably younger than my sister, bounded out the front door, and down the steps to meet us. He opened Renni's door and they hugged even before she stepped out of the Jeep.

By the time I got out, he had come around to greet me as warmly as he had her. "You must be Kiki," I said, freeing myself from his enthusiastic embrace.

"Bertrand, really," he said. "She calls me Kiki because I'm born and raised in Waikiki," he laughed, nodding in Renni's direction. An all-black Great Dane befitting royalty ran up to me barking, but also wagging his long tail.

"What a beautiful dog," I said, thinking about Pee-Pee, its opposite in every way. "Is he friendly?"

"She," Renni corrected. "Her name's LSD, but we call her Lucy. Yeah, she's friendly, unless you're afraid of being licked to death."

I crouched, and she put her jowly muzzle in my face. Her single, sloppy kiss traveled from my chin to my forehead, a proper welcome.

Kiki took my bag and led me first into the upstairs part of the house with its magnificent wraparound windows. We walked into a spacious, wide-open living room. They kept the interior lights to a bare minimum, and the panoramic view took my breath away.

"Hungry?" he asked.

"More exhausted than hungry," I said. It was close to seven o'clock here, which meant it was approaching ten o'clock in Oakland, and I was fading.

"You'll feel better after a good meal," he said, as if my answer to his first question were irrelevant.

"So, you own a fleet of yachts, I hear," I said, adding my own irrelevant follow-up.

A loud laugh burst from his mouth as he said, "Yachts! That's funny. You've been listening to the wrong person. What I own is five catamarans. I'll take you out on one whenever you'd like."

I was liking him more and more.

Renni came in behind us. "Take Shorty downstairs and show him what we've got for him," she said, and then turned to give me another hug. I followed Kiki down a spiral staircase just off the living room, and found myself in one of the nicest apartments I'd ever seen. Like the upstairs, it was designed for maximum space, open and airy. Kiki led me to an ample bedroom in the back with two large windows, though the view from downstairs was no match for the mind-blowing view upstairs. He put my bag down on the double bed, covered by a deep blue quilt. He showed me the bathroom, and asked if I wanted to take a shower before heading out to dinner. I could definitely use a shower, but I decided I needed sleep even more, so I just said, "No. Let's go."

The Porsche was apparently a two-seater, because we piled back into the Jeep for the drive into Waikiki. At the entrance to the Royal Hawaiian, Renni handed the keys over to a young valet, maybe Chinese or Japanese, maybe Filipino or Hawaiian or Samoan – or, more likely, some blended combination.

We chose a table outside where the sound of the waves competed with those from the nightly luau the tourists paid $85 per head to attend. We could see the nearly naked men on the stage gyrating to the sound of ukeleles and drums. The light of tiki torches reflected off their glistening bodies. I had never experienced anything like this.

A beautiful young woman, wearing little more than the male dancers, brought us a menu, and I scanned it quickly.

"What's a pupu,"I asked, and thought again of Pee-Pee.

Kiki laughed, but Renni said, "I'll do the ordering for all of us. Don't worry."

"Yeah, but what's a pupu," I asked again. The setting itself, the surf, the dancers, the incredible luxury, all conspired to revive my appetite.

"Hors d'oeuvres" she said carefully, as if it were a word I might not be familiar with. "They're appetizers," she added, just in case.

Appetizers like Hawaiian Sweet Chile Baby Ribs for $14.75, or Hamachi Sashimi for $19.50. Under the "Main Courses" category, I found Baked Macadamia Nut Crusted Fijian Butterfish ($33.25), whose description didn't live up to its name: "Pineapple Fried Rice, Sautéed Baby Bok Choy, Orange Sauce."

When the waitress returned, Renni ordered two different pupu dishes, Blue Lump Crab Cake ($21) and Coconut Fried Shrimp ($17.75). "How are you with lobster," she asked, as if lobster and I were in a relationship.

"Take it or leave it," I said, "But if I get to order ice cream for dessert, I'll leave all the other choices to you."

"Still an ice cream freak, huh," she said, shaking her head. She never had liked the cold confection, which was a boon to me when we were children. I always got hers, or at least some of hers.

She turned back to the waitress. "We'll have the Maple Leaf Duck Cooked Two-Ways," she said, reading from the menu. "Also, the Dynamite Crab Crusted Mahi Mahi, and three Royal Ono Ono salads." As she ordered, I quickly calculated the cost from the menu in front of me. Those two entrees alone, along with the three salads, would set her back more than $125, and that was before the expensive bottle of wine she ordered, and the desserts that would follow. But that was nothing to Renni.

"So?" she asked. The pupus came, and then the salad, as I gave them a thumbnail sketch of how my life had been turned upside down, and what I was hoping to find in Honolulu.

"Why?" my sister asked. And there it was again.

"I guess that's the question I want to answer," I said. "Why did he do it? I'm not sure why I need to know, but I need to know."

An older Chinese man bussed the appetizer and salad dishes, clearing the table for the waitress who came and put the duck and fish platters in the middle of it, spooning out decent portions on each of our plates, and leaving the rest for us to choose from. Kiki said little during the meal, and Renni seemed satisfied with my vague answer to the "why" question. Instead of pursuing the subject, she gave me a rundown of her own Hawaiian activities, which included diving, snorkeling, and Samoan dancing. Her descriptions were peppered with funny little anecdotes, like the time her diving instructor had tried to dissuade her from a particularly deep dive because of her age. She told him she thought he was too young to give such advice, and then dove deeper than everyone else. "I actually speared an octopus," she said, triumphantly, "and learned to cook it, too."

The dessert menu came, and I ordered Pineapple Upside Down Cake with koloa rum ice cream, macadamia nuts, and burnt brown sugar butter (another $13.50). This was indulgent extravagance, but I was not protesting. By the time we stuffed our stuffed selves back into the Jeep, I was ready for sleep. Renni chattered happily all the way back to Blue Point, where the Jeep's headlights caught Lucy's green eyes as she came running toward us in anticipation of being loved by all.

I kissed my sister, who handed me a key to the downstairs apartment, shook Kiki's hand, and went down the outside stairs to my comfortable new digs. I was extremely tired, but the private beach Renni had shown me before dinner, just twenty yards from their back entrance, and the lure of a nighttime swim in ocean waters warm enough to bathe in, was too strong to resist. I undressed, and found

Butch's business card in my pocket. It was straightforward enough, with his name in bold black letters, TED PAULSON, under which, in smaller letters, were the words: Editor, *Honolulu Times-Bulletin*. There was a phone number in the lower right-hand corner.

I'm not even sure why, but I dialed the number on the old-fashioned pink Princess phone on the bed stand. I expected an electronic message telling me that the paper was closed for the night. Instead, the man I had known as a boy said, "Hello," on the second ring.

"Butch," I said. Then, quickly, "Ted, I mean. I'm sorry. Ted. This is Harrison Ovitz."

"Yes," he said. "I recognize your voice."

"I just wanted to apologize for my sister," I began, but he cut me off as sharply as Renni had cut him off at the baggage carousel.

"No," he said. "Please. No. You don't owe me an apology at all. You don't owe me anything but contempt for how I treated you. I'm just grateful for the opportunity to apologize to you."

"Can we meet and talk about it?" I asked, surprising myself.

"I'd like that," he said. "Can I take you to breakfast? Lunch? Or we could just meet for a drink."

"I don't know Honolulu at all," I said, "and I don't know what my sister has planned. But breakfast sounds good."

"Can I pick you up, say around nine tomorrow morning," he offered.

"Do you know where Blue Point is?" I asked.

"Everyone knows where Blue Point is," he chuckled. "It's got one of the most fantastic views of any place on the island."

"I was about to go for a swim. Want to join me?"

"That is an extremely generous offer," he said. "I truly regret that I can't accept it tonight. Another time, yes, but not tonight. I'd really like to share a meal with you, though."

"Tomorrow, then," I said. 'We're the very last house at the end of the road. And don't be put off by the dog. She's as loving as she is big."

"Nine o'clock," he replied. "We'll have a real Hawaiian breakfast. You do like Spam, I hope." And he chuckled again before hanging up.

The conversation, brief as it was, had buoyed me as little else had in days. I put on my trunks, and trotted down to the water. Gingerly, I put a toe into the surf. The air was cool, which made the water seem even warmer than it was, and I waded out waist-deep before plunging in fully, swimming easily away from the shore.

I lay on my back, bobbing gently in the warm water. This was something I could get used to. I was close enough to the shore to see the lights from Renni's house, and the jagged crown of Diamond Head aglow from the lights of Waikiki beyond. I could hear the waves as they broke on the white sand shore, and the shushing sound they made as they rushed back into the sea, as soothing as a Brahms' lullaby. I felt completely relaxed for the first time since my trauma – Soul Man's trauma – on the Bridge. I bobbed and rolled effortlessly in the ocean's natural rhythms. In that confluence of wonderfully warm water, its perpetual motion making its own music, and the magnificence of the moonless night sky that spread out above me like a canopy, a black canvas brilliantly lit by a billion stars, I felt tears come to my eyes. Whatever tomorrow might bring, the incomparable now was everything.

# Chapter Eighteen

I woke when it was not yet light, though not quite dark. I sat up, forgetting for a moment where I was before rousing myself. I hadn't had a chance to tell Renni about my breakfast plans, but I had more than a couple of hours before Ted was scheduled to pick me up. I heard nothing from upstairs, so I decided not to disturb them. Instead, I grabbed a towel and opted for an early morning swim.

Unlike my experience the night before, this was much more routine, swimming out from the beach perhaps twenty-five yards or so, and then doing the equivalent of laps parallel to the shore. When I encountered a pod of seven dolphins arching through the surf as far from me as I was from the shore, I realized that a "routine swim" in these spectacular waters was anything but routine. I watched them leap out of the water as one, like a display of synchronized swimmers at the Olympics. Gold Medalists! They showed no interest in me, and I have no idea if they were even aware of my presence. Soon, they swam out to sea and out of sight.

I back-stroked in, dried off, and went back to my room to shower and dress. It was closer to eight than to seven when I made my way upstairs to find Renni in the kitchen with the makings of breakfast on the counter: a dozen eggs, a see-through package labeled Portuguese Sausage, two large avocados and a colorful variety of fruits I couldn't identify.

"Morning, Beautiful," I said as I entered the room. I could smell the coffee brewing, and I wanted some. "Can I help myself to coffee?"

"Only way you're gonna get some," Renni answered. "Cups are in that cupboard over there," she pointed. "It's Kona coffee, the world's best."

I poured myself a cup, took a sip, and decided it wasn't the world's best, but best to keep my mouth shut on that score.

"Delicious," I said. "Where's Kiki?"

"He had some meeting in Hilo this morning," she said. "Took the first flight out. He left an hour ago. You ready for breakfast?"

Instead of answering her directly, I told her about the dolphins, which didn't impress her at all.

"Oh, yeah, there are a lot of them off the Point," she said. "What about breakfast?"

"Uh, well... Don't get mad, Sis, but I have been invited out to breakfast."

"Who by," she laughed, "the dolphins?"

"I wouldn't mind that," I said, "but actually it's Ted."

"Who?"

"Ted. We met him at the airport yesterday."

"You're not talking about the asshole, I hope."

"None other," I replied as off-handedly as I could, trying to limit her reaction. "We talked on the phone briefly last night, and he invited me for a typical Hawaiian breakfast this morning. He's picking me up in less than an hour."

"I don't believe it. On our first day together? You're like milk toast," she snorted in my direction. "You should flatten the fucker, not go out to breakfast with him. I hope you like Spam," she nearly spat.

"That's just what he said."

Renni made an elaborate show of preparing her breakfast in silence, while I nursed a second cup of good – not great – coffee, and tried to re-engage her in conversation. But she wouldn't have it. She wanted me to know how hurt she was, and studiously avoided all my lame efforts.

"So, Sis, who watches your Taos mansion when you're here?"

She chopped the sausage savagely, by way of an answer, giving me the impression that she wished it were Ted's neck – or mine – under the butcher knife.

"What's on your agenda for today," I tried again.

The sound of eggs being beaten furiously.

"Can I pour you a cup of coffee?"

She poured her own.

"Okay," I conceded. "You're mad. You have a right... You think you might be over it any time soon?"

Nothing.

"I'm going out on the veranda to enjoy this delicious coffee," I said. "The conversation is better out there."

"It's called a lanai," she corrected, "not a veranda."

"Ah. You're talking to me."

"No, I'm not," she said.

I retreated to a deck chair on the lanai and breathed in the sweet air, already warmed by the brilliant sun, which had only risen an hour or so before. I didn't mind Renni's cold shoulder. I knew it wouldn't last long. By the time I got back, whenever that might be, she would have forgotten her pique, presenting me with eager new plans for the afternoon or evening or next day. She could erupt like a Hawaiian volcano; she could be brutal in her denunciations; but she didn't have it in her to sustain those emotions over time. It was, in fact, one of her best qualities. She told me once, "If I carried around all the grudges I develop in a day, I'd weigh too much to walk."

As much as Renni hoped to make me feel guilty, it would take a lot more than her silence to bring me down; swimming with the dolphins had made sure of that. When Ted knocked on the door, I jumped to get there first, but not fast enough. Renni opened the door.

"Okay, Shit Head," she said by way of greeting, but lightly, without the malice that she had displayed the day before. "I have just one question: when will you return him to me?" She cocked her head to one side, as if to add "Hmm?" to her question. I relaxed, as I'm sure Ted did, too.

"Well," he answered, smiling, "I was hoping to take him to the Beach Park at Waimea, which means we probably won't get back 'til after three or four. Is that all right?"

"Of course it's not all right," she replied in mock anger, bantering with my old nemesis. "But you men folk are in charge, so you go ahead and do whatever it is you men folk do, and be back in time for dinner. And never mind that I wanted to take him to Waimea."

"We could go somewhere else," he replied, a gentle gift offering.

"Are you kidding," she said. "I don't think there's a place on this island you could take him that I wouldn't wish to take him first."

"I love being fought over like this," I interjected.

"Shut up," Renni ordered. "Be back in time for dinner. And that's both of you. Now get out of here."

"Aloha," Ted said, offering Renni his hand. As she took it, she couldn't resist adding, "I hope you know you'll probably be Shit Head forever to me, unless you compliment my cooking. If you do that, I'll consider calling you Ted."

She remembered his name, had taken his hand, received his aloha, and invited him to dinner. I wished I had her facility to go from fury to forgiveness so easily. I didn't, but I was particularly grateful this morning that she did.

Ted and I drove away in his ancient Nash Rambler, a 45-year-old relic of a car that, judging by how well it looked, he obviously loved. It had a gold-colored body with a black roof and trim. It became the focus of our initial small talk.

"You like old cars," I said. "It rides great."

"No, not really. I just like the look of the Rambler. I do like working on it, though."

Our chitchat about insignificant things carried us through much denser freeway traffic than I had imagined for Hawaii, and then up and over a steep mountain road that led to the other side of the island. At the top, there was an overlook where we parked, joining other tourists standing at the edge of the cliff. I soon added my own oohs and aahs to theirs. The panoramic view of Honolulu below and the sparkling Pacific Ocean beyond – wow!

I'm not sure why I took this sightseeing moment to ask, "Ted, how did you...?" My question trailed off in the wind, but he was reading my mind.

"How did I stop being the asshole I was?" he said.

"That's not how I would have put it," I said, "but, yeah."

"Therapy," he answered. "Therapy," he repeated, "and lots of it."

I didn't say much of anything for quite a while as we drove on, except to comment on the unfolding beauty of the island, the sea on one side and the lava-rock mountains on the other. I tried to pronounce the strange names of the small towns we drove through.

"Kaaawa," I'd say.

"No," he would say, "not Kaaawa, but Ka'a'ava." And there were others like Hau'ula, La'ie and Kawela.

In Hau'ula, he pulled into a narrow parking area next to a nondescript little wooden shack-like building with a hand-carved sign over the entrance announcing Papa Ono's Kitchen. There was a "Cash Only" sign on the door and half a dozen picnic tables out front, one of which remained unoccupied until we grabbed it.

"Is this going to be my Spam breakfast," I asked, still wanting to pursue his path to therapy, but not knowing how to get there.

"If you like Spam. It's on the menu. But order whatever you want. It's on me," Ted said.

I had to ask him what most of the items on the menu were, items like laulau (pork wrapped in taro leaves), lomi-lomi (cubed pieces of raw salmon in a spicy sauce), and loco moco (white rice topped with a fried egg and hamburger, all smothered in a brown savory gravy).

"What's poke?" I asked.

"Poki," he corrected, laughing. "It's raw tuna in soy sauce. Ono."

"Ono?"

"Delicious," he said.

He ordered the loco moco, but I opted for something less adventuresome: sweet bread French toast. I had to ask, first, if it had anything to do with sweetbreads, like I'd eaten once in San Francisco and discovered, sadly, were neither sweet nor bread. "If that's what it is," I said, "then typical Hawaiian breakfast or not, I ain't eatin' it!"

Ted laughed, and I laughed with him.

"No," he said. "It's actually sweet Portuguese bread, dipped in a custard batter and deep fried."

"Ono," I said.

"Ono," he agreed.

When the French toast was served, I had to ask more questions about the fruit piled on the plate.

"What's this," I asked, tasting a deliciously tart jelly that adorned the six slices of fruit-covered toast.

"Lilikoi," he said. "Passion fruit. It's an acquired taste for some."

"Never heard of it," I said, licking my fingers, "but I've already acquired a taste." *It would make wonderful ice cream*, I thought.

As we ate, Ted pressed me for details about the mission I was on. He asked if I minded if he took notes.

"Almost forgot," I said, "you're the newspaper editor, aren't you?"

"A newspaper editor," he corrected, stressing the first word, "not the newspaper editor. But there might be a story in this, if you don't mind."

He jotted down some basic information about my quest, especially Soul Man's deep dive into oblivion that had set it all in motion. But strangely – at least to me – he seemed far more interested in my work on behalf of abused children, asking probing questions about how F.A.C.T. had come into existence, my role in the organization, and details about the upcoming annual fundraising Dinner. Which reminded me, this would be the first such Dinner I would miss since taking the job. At the same moment, I realized I didn't miss missing it.

"Do you mind if I try to turn this into a piece for the paper," he asked, as he paid the bill.

"Fine with me," I said, "if you think anyone would be interested."

We kept driving for another half hour or so, with me answering more of his questions, but wishing I could find an opening to ask him the questions his confession about therapy had ignited in me.

When we pulled into the parking area at Waimea Beach Park, I understood instantly why both he and my sister wanted to show off this place – a Hawaiian picture postcard. It had a huge white-sand beach with palm trees providing shade. There were whole families cavorting in the surf, and couples whose male halves wore the briefest of briefs and whose female halves lay face down with bra straps untied, soaking up the rays they hoped would turn them brown or browner. At the foot of this wide expanse was the ocean whose great waves – dwarfing anything I'd seen up to now – gathered and crashed onto the shore. And suspended in those gathering walls of glass-clear water were the bodies of swimmers, held upright as the wave passed over them, like living statues. I had never seen anything like it.

"Shoulda brought my trunks," I said, as we settled ourselves at an empty picnic table under a tree with red paintbrush-like flowers.

"I've got extra trunks in my trunk," he riffed, adding, "You learn quickly around here to always be ready to go into the water."

"Maybe later," I said. "Remember what our mothers said? We just ate..." Ted laughed out loud at that.

We sat in silence for a while. Well, not silence really, only silence between us. The sound of children squealing in delight, of noisy mynah birds jumping from palm frond to palm frond, of huge waves thundering their demise on the shore were reasons enough for our silence.

I was the first to speak. "What the heck is that," I asked, pointing to a sleek, sinewy brown animal moving along the top of a rock wall just behind us. "Is that a weasel?"

"No, it's a mongoose," Ted answered. I thought of Rikki-Tikki-Tavi, the cobra killer in Rudyard Kipling's *Just So* stories that my mother had read to Renni and me when my sister was still Irene.

"Huh," I said. "Sure looks like a weasel."

"Not the weasel I remember," Ted said, mysteriously. Was this the opening I was hoping for, I wondered. I said nothing; neither did Ted for a minute. And then he took a deep breath, as if he were about to dive under one of those waves. "Did you ever meet my Uncle Weasel," he asked.

"Uncle Weasel? Was that his real name?"

"No. It's just what my brother and I called him. It's what he was."

"I didn't know you had a brother," I said. "To be honest, I wasn't that interested in hearing about your family when we were in school."

"Yeah, right," he said, nodding his head. "Yeah, right," he repeated, thinking back. "Well, I had a brother. Older than me. He killed himself when I was in prison."

I know I should have expressed some kind of condolence for his brother, but the words just popped out: "In prison," I exclaimed.

"In prison," he replied impassively, as if reading from a guide book. "Ronnie – my brother Ronald – he couldn't deal with it. Going to prison saved my life."

"Couldn't deal with what," I asked.

"Uncle Weasel."

"Why? What did he do?"

"He preyed on us when we were too small and too stupid to protect ourselves. First Ronnie, then me. Ronnie tried to tell our dad about it, and for that he was rewarded with a beating. I guess it was more important to protect his brother than his children."

This was unchartered territory for me. You'd think someone whose job it is to raise money to protect children from sexual abuse would know what to do when confronted by it, but I didn't. Oh, I knew all the statistics. I knew the research showing that one in six boys and one in five girls were routinely sexually abused before the age of 16. I remembered a quote from a study released the year before concluding that male childhood sexual abuse was "common, under reported, under-recognized, and undertreated." And I knew that most of the perpetrators were family members or friends of the family.

What I didn't know was what to say to someone who had experienced this grossest betrayal of all. I had no trouble raising money on behalf of the victims of such betrayal, but could not raise the words that might provide a modicum of comfort. They stuck in my throat, though platitudes covered my own inadequacy.

"I'm so sorry," I said. Those were the only words I was able to utter, as if suffering from crippling emotional paralysis. And so I repeated, "I'm so sorry."

"No," Ted said. "Don't be sorry. I was powerless to stop what was happening to me, so I took it out on you. And not just you. Everybody."

He paused, looking off into the distance.

"But you got therapy," I finally managed to say.

"Not by choice," he said.

"How did you get it then," I asked.

He sighed heavily. "Prison," he said. "I went to prison because I found my power in beating my wife."

"You're married?"

"I was. No more. It really didn't last long," he continued. "She was not the kind of woman who accepted her fate in silence. She called the cops the first time it happened, and the D.A. got a domestic violence conviction against me. At the time, I hated all of it. I hated her for turning me in. I hated the D.A. for going after me. I guess I hated myself most of all. Always hated myself..."

Again, his voice trailed off into distant memories, of which I had no knowledge. "Of course, I hated prison, too," he went on. "The only reason I joined that group of men in the prison therapy unit was that it got me out of my cell. At first, I hated the group, too, but it was better than sitting behind that locked steel door."

Almost involuntarily, I put my hand on Ted's arm, adding this impotent gesture to my impotent words. "I'm so sorry."

"No," he repeated. "I found enlightenment among those damaged men. I learned something that you probably already know because of your work. I'm not saying that every boy who's been molested grows up to be an abuser, but every man in that group, every abusive man in that group had experienced some form of what I had experienced. Every last one of them."

*Who are the people we think we know*, I wondered. How do we presume to judge people when all we know of them are those moments when their lives interact with ours. I knew I hated Butch in middle school, hated being the object of his torture, hated being the indirect object of his torturer, though I had no idea he had one. Yes, I hated him, but I really didn't know him at all.

"I was a fucking asshole," he said. "I knew I was even then. I just didn't know why until those sessions at Soledad. I didn't know. I am so, so sorry." Somehow, the same impotent words I had spoken to him came back to me. And now, they had real power, and I felt it. For the first time, his voice broke, and suddenly, I felt the tears jump into my own eyes, tears that I must have been holding back since the 7$^{th}$ grade, because now they came. They came, and I could not hold them back. I'm ashamed to say that I wept like a child. I wept not just for my own pain, and not just for Ted's, but for all of it – the inescapable pain of being human.

And just as suddenly, Ted was holding me, and I continued to cry. This man who seemed to have no connection to the boy I thought I knew, the boy I hated, my former tormentor was trying to comfort me now – and it was working.

It took more time than I'd care to admit for me to get control of myself. Ted loosened his embrace, an embrace that meant so much more than the hugs of my sister and her boyfriend the day before.

"I didn't know," I said, wiping my tears on my sleeve.

"I didn't either," he said. "It took a long time. I knew what my uncle did to us, but not what it meant, not how it stunted my development. Now I do, though. Now I do, and I'm so very sorry."

For a moment, we sat there.

"Let's go for a swim," Ted suggested, breaking our silence. He retrieved a pair of trunks for me and one for himself, and we went into the cement shower room to change. We raced down to the water, wading in waist high before diving under a giant wave that broke above us. For half an hour, we frolicked like children, sometimes diving below the waves, sometimes letting their power carry us onto the wet sand before jumping back in. For those few minutes, we were boys again, trying to recapture a time in our lives that we'd never had. Like the tears that had so unexpectedly sprung from some deep well inside me, laughter now animated our late-blooming adolescent friendship. *Maybe the lesson is no more profound than that people change*, I thought, as I came up holding my breath, and squirted him with a mouthful of salt water.

We showered, dried using the one towel he carried, and headed back to the car.

"You know how to drive a stick," he asked.

"Doesn't everybody," I answered.

"Good. Do you mind driving? I'd like to get my notes in order so I can dictate a story to the copy editor when we get back."

"I'm not sure I know the way," I protested as I adjusted the seat to accommodate my long legs.

"I'm right next to you," he said. "You won't get lost."

# Chapter Nineteen

Ted sat on the edge of my bed, using the little Princess phone to call in his story while I showered for dinner. And what a dinner! Renni completely outdid herself, and there was nothing fake about the comp-liments the three men around the table heaped on her.

"That's called Hapu'up'u," she said, placing a steaming platter in the middle of the table on which sat a whole, huge fish. "Grouper," Kiki said. The platter itself was a work of art, but so was the fish, garnished with small curled ends of scallions and generously peppered with ginger and macadamia nuts.

"And it's as fresh as the sea," Renni added. "While you were out gallivanting, I did a deep dive and came up with this little sucker."

"No you didn't," Kiki laughed. "Stop taking credit for my catch."

"Well," Renni replied, "you're my catch, so indirectly I'm responsible."

"How do you make those green onions curl up like that," Ted asked.

"Oh, so easy," Renni explained. "Just cut 'em the size you want and soak 'em in ice water. They do the rest. And they do look nice, don't they?"

"You must have been cooking all day to prepare a feast like this," Ted continued. No doubt, Renni knew she was being buttered up, but she loved it.

"Try some of the sweet and sour sausage rice," she beamed. She had prepared a culinary masterpiece that made me question my usual ice cream-only diet. In addition to the steaming fish and sausage rice, she identified the other dishes surrounding the platter as a stir-fry called "drunken eggplant," an incredibly delicious mango black bean salad, and Parmesan garlic toasted flatbread.

"There's dessert," she cautioned, filling our wine glasses with an expensive Australian shiraz, "so leave room."

Conversation flowed, no doubt enhanced by the shiraz and the coconut-flavored Hawaiian rum liqueur Renni served with the key lime margarita pie she'd made for dessert. Of course, we had not followed her advice to "leave room," but somehow we made room, stuffing our already stuffed selves.

By the time Ted was ready to go home, he and my sister were talking like old friends.

"You'll spend Christmas with us, won't you Ted?"

Christmas! Except for the reminder of that incongruous red bow Renni had tied around Lucy's huge neck, I had hardly remembered the season at all. Christmas Eve was the next day.

"No presents is our rule," Renni added. But what she really meant was that only she was allowed to give presents, which she did freely – except never on Christmas day. It was like a religious thing with her, or, more accurately, an anti-religious thing.

"No presents, no Christmas tree, no phony snow. You'll come for breakfast and stay all day. We'll play charades, drink, swim, talk, whatever. You have to come."

"Oh, I'll be here," Ted said, smiling broadly.

When Ted left, I went downstairs, and decided to phone Perry for an update. I hadn't yet told him about Ted, or the story he was writing, and I didn't know if the SFPD had made any progress identifying whoever it was Soul Man had been talking to before his flight into oblivion ended that call.

"What's up in Paradise," Perry asked after we exchanged helloes, and bantered a bit about Lilla, the girls and, of course, Pee-Pee. I told him about the article Ted was hoping to see in today's paper. "Fucking A," he said, pleased with himself for having pointed the way. "If it gets published, that could pay major dividends," he added.

"Yeah, unless your buddies across the Bay have already traced that call, and can tell you who it was. Then we wouldn't have to worry about dividends. The D.A. said they could trace it."

"Right," Perry said in his most sarcastic voice. "You really think they're going to put resources into a suicide? Maybe if someone had pushed him, but a suicide? And a Black man, at that? You're barking up the wrong tree if you're waiting for them to find anything more than we've already found. Even if it had been a murder," he said, "it'd probably take them months before remembering that a phone call initiated this whole thing. No, my friend. It's all up to you now," Perry added.

It wasn't the update I was hoping for. It didn't make for a good night's sleep.

*****

Renni woke me up early Christmas Eve morning. I hadn't even heard the phone ring. "It's Ted," she said. "He sounds pretty excited."

I cleared my throat before picking up the receiver. "Morning, Ted," I said, hoping I didn't sound too groggy.

"Sorry for calling so early," he said, skipping the usual phone pleasantries, "but you're gonna wanna know about this."

"What's that," I asked, swinging my legs over the side of the bed and sitting up.

"The piece ran on the front page of the local news section this morning."

"Great."

"More than great," he said. "I got a call this morning. Someone who thinks she knows who you're looking for."

That did it. I was completely awake now. "What'd she say?" I asked.

"There's an officer that everyone calls the Pearl of Pearl Harbor. A Navy captain. An African American Navy captain. An African American Navy captain named Pearley."

*How many Pearleys are stationed at Pearl Harbor*, I wondered.

"Did you get her last name?"

"Arlington. Captain Pearley Arlington."

"Is there any way we can get on base to talk to her?"

"I'm pretty sure I can get that done," Ted said. "I did a piece on base security a while back. I know the P.I.O. I think he'll let me take you to see her if I explain why."

I felt more than a little stupid when I had to ask what a P.I.O. is. "Public Information Officer," Ted explained. Duh.

"What can I do?" I asked.

"You've already done it. It's all in the article. Let me give a call and see if I can set things up. I'll call you back."

I took a quick shower and went upstairs. Renni was slicing a papaya on the counter. "I figured half a papaya would do for breakfast after how much we packed away last night," she said. "I can make you eggs or anything else if you're up to it. I don't know how he did it, but Kiki ate a full breakfast before leaving this morning."

"The papaya and a cup of coffee will do just fine," I said.

"Me too," she said. "What did Ted want," she asked as she poured our coffee. I explained what had happened.

"Is there a place nearby where I can get a paper?" I asked.

"Not exactly nearby," she said. "There's a small market a couple of miles from here. You can get one there. Let's eat and I'll take you."

"Do you mind if we get the paper first and eat afterwards?"

"What a demanding guest you are," she complained, then kissed me on the forehead. By the time we got back, I had read the article twice. It began dramatically with Soul Man's swan dive, but quickly turned into a description of F.A.C.T., including more than one reference to the big Dinner, which was only three days away. Renni's answer machine was blinking, a message from Ted.

"Call me," the disembodied voice said.

"We're in," he said, as soon as he picked up the phone. "I'll pick you up at eleven. They're having a formal Dress Parade after lunch, so we won't have a lot of time with her."

When I told Renni, she said, "You're not going to just turn around and go back to Oakland if you find her, are you?" There was a quality in her voice that surprised me.

"Don't know, Sis. I haven't thought that far ahead." But I understood that the question she had asked me was not an idle one. She wasn't being a polite hostess. She wasn't flattering my ego. She really wanted me to stay.

"You know you can stay here as long as you want," she added.

There was no doubt that Renni could afford to keep me, but the thought of being kept – of living off my sister – didn't sit right. Everything about the place made me want to stay, but doing so on my sister's dime wasn't in my DNA.

She was uncharacteristically quiet after that. She squeezed a wedge of lime onto both halves of the papaya, and put one of them in front of me.

"Ono," I said, and she smiled and nodded.

Finally, she said, "I hope it's not her. I hope you don't find her. Not today, anyway. Not so soon."

"Don't say that, Sis. I have to find her. I have to know if he was talking to her when he went over the side. I can't explain why I have to know, but I have to know. It's almost all I'm able to think about. I have to know. Do you understand?"

"No... yes. Yes, I understand. Do you understand why I don't want you to?"

There were tears in Renni's eyes when she asked me this, a rarity. She had seen me cry often enough, but I had hardly ever seen her cry. I reached over and took her hand. She squeezed as a single tear spilled over the causeway of her lower lid.

# Chapter Twenty

"Do you believe in God?" Ted asked me as the Rambler made its way through traffic.

"That's a strange question," I said. "What made you ask?"

He was silent for a moment before answering. "I don't know. It's just that we're here. We've arrived at this place totally separately, and yet we're here, together. And I like you."

"I like you, too," I said. "I really do. But I'm not sure how much evidence that is for God's existence."

"So you don't believe in some higher intelligence?" he pressed.

"Oh, I do," I said. "Half the people I know have higher intelligence than me. Look at you, for example."

Ted laughed. "Oh, please, give me a break."

"It's tempting," I said. "To believe in God, I mean. I just can't bring myself there. I guess I've seen too much human cruelty, too much injustice, too many children hurt and hurting, like you. I can't believe in any cosmic intelligence when the world seems so overcome with ignorance."

"So, you think it's just coincidence that we've hooked up as friends after starting so long ago as enemies?"

"Yes," I answered. "I believe in coincidence. What about you?"

"I'm still working on that one," he said.

The conversation ended at the entrance to Pearl Harbor. Two uniformed petty officers, a man and a woman, dressed almost identically in beige, stood as sentries. The woman asked Ted what we wanted. When he mentioned the name of the P.I.O., the man went into a small booth and looked at a clipboard hanging on the wall. When he returned, he asked for Ted's ID, then mine.

"You know where you're going?" he asked.

"Aye aye, Sir," Ted couldn't resist saying as we passed into the base under a green banner with red lettering that spelled out MELE

KALIKIMAKA. We passed a long line of tourists at a different nearby entrance, waiting for their $95 tour of the USS Arizona in its watery grave. We parked in a visitor's spot close to one where a sign read, "Reserved for Public Information Officer," and entered his small office.

He told us that Captain Arlington was waiting for us in her office, and assured us that he had told her nothing of the purpose of our visit. My hands had already begun to sweat in anticipation. He directed us to another building where the Captain's office was.

Leaving the car where we parked it, we walked briskly toward the building that housed her office. "I'm scared to death," I said, surprising even myself.

"Of what?" Ted asked. "Are you more scared that it will be her or that it won't?" I let the question hang in the air, unanswered. The truth was that I didn't know the answer.

When we found the building, a nondescript cement block structure, we had to ask a sailor where the Captain's office was. We found it in the basement of the building, a corner office. On the door was a sign announcing: Captain Phylicia Arlington. Phylicia with a Ph.

"Phylicia? I thought your informant said her name was Pearley."

"That's what she told me," Ted said. "Or, at least, that's what they call her."

We stood outside the door for a minute. I wiped my hands on my trousers, looked at Ted, and knocked twice. Immediately came the one-word command: "Enter."

# Chapter Twenty-One

Captain Arlington was seated behind a heavy wooden desk with several neat piles of paper on it. Like the door itself, a name plate identified her as Captain Phylicia Arlington. She was dark-skinned, with short-cropped hair more salt than pepper, an impressive-looking woman of, perhaps 50, or so. The deep blue uniform she wore with its gold stripes on both sleeves and a row of brass buttons down the front of her, gave her an extra air of authority. She sported an impressive display of ribbons and medals on the left side of her lapel.

Behind her stood two flags, one of the Stars and Stripes, the other depicting the Navy emblem, a picture of an eagle in the foreground and a tall-masted ship behind. On the wall behind the flags a full-length portrait of President Clinton looked down, alongside the face of another white man I took to be the Secretary of the Navy.

"Gentlemen," she said, and bid us to take a seat, which we did. "Would you care for some coffee? A soft drink?" There was a controlled quality to her diction. She enunciated each word in a precise, clipped way, an adopted manner of speech that she had perfected, and which conferred an additional degree of dignity. When we declined her offer of refreshments, she continued. "The P.I.O. gave me very little information about your visit, so can you enlighten me?"

Ted spoke first. "My name is Ted Paulson," he said. "I write for the *Times-Bulletin*. This is my good friend, Harrison Ovitz." She turned her gaze on me, as if waiting for me to say something.

"I thought your name was Pearley," I said. I hadn't planned on saying that. It just sort of came out. But, at least, we would know if we should turn around and start over.

"Who told you my name was Pearley?" she asked, looking puzzled.

"I've been looking for a woman named Pearley," I said, as if that explained everything. "Someone told us they call you the Pearl of Pearl Harbor."

She laughed at this. "Well, I can assure you that no one calls me that to my face. As it happens, though, my first name is Pearl. To be precise, it's Pearley, but there aren't many alive who can get away with calling me that."

Ted and I exchanged glances.

"I use my middle name, Phylicia," she said, and then, "My time is rather limited, gentlemen, so how can I help you?"

*She hasn't seen the article*, I thought with a feeling of relief. But I immediately regretted that feeling as my brain caught up with the reality that she, Captain Pearley Phylicia Arlington, was almost certainly the person I was searching for. She hadn't read the article, so she didn't know her husband – ex-husband, I figured – had killed himself, and it would be my job to tell her.

"Do you know a man named Joshua Jeppards?" I asked, plunging into the deep end of the pool.

The change in her demeanor came instantly. Her whole body stiffened, and the expression on her face froze. "Did he send you to find me?" she asked, in that same controlled way.

"Yeah. Sort of. You could say he sent me."

"Well, I'm sending you back."

I turned to Ted. "Do you have the newspaper?" He pulled a copy from his backpack and handed it to her across the desk. For the next few minutes, she read silently, looking up from time to time and shaking her head. Finally, she read aloud from the article:

"They looked into each other's eyes before Mr. Jeppards jumped over the side of the Bridge to his death." She looked up and added her own editorial comment. "The act of a coward," she said.

Coward is not a word I would have used to describe Soul Man. "Because he wouldn't carry live ammunition like a slave while white officers made bets on him? Because he served time in prison?" I asked, defensively.

"No," she said, calmly but firmly, "that is not what I was referring to."

Now, she looked directly at me. Her eyes seemed both to accuse and to sympathize at the same time. She slid the newspaper back across the desk to us. "It says you work for an organization that helps children who've been abused. Is that right?"

"Well, I was a fundraiser for them, yes."

"And that you've been haunted by Mr. Jeppards' suicide for... how long?"

"Days," I said. "Weeks. It feels like forever."

How was it that I was now answering her questions, rather than the other way around? Irrationally, I thought of Renni, and how very different she was in demeanor from the Naval officer now asking me questions. Renni dealt with life in a lighthearted way, even when things got serious. The woman now sitting across the desk from us was as light-hearted as a funeral, and one got the impression that even when things were not serious, that was how she dealt with life. Yet, both women had the power to take control of a situation, a quality which often put me at odds with my sister but which, I was sure, made Captain Arlington a first-rate officer.

"Some weeks," she repeated. "Do you know how long I have been haunted by that man?"

Perhaps it was the word "haunted" that put me back on the Bridge, shivering in fear of what was coming. Ted and I sat there, mute, as she calmly answered her own question. "Forever," she said. "All my life."

Just as I had felt that death was near at hand when Soul Man's eyes met mine that cold, early morning, now I felt a premonition that I was about to learn something I did not want to know. The distinct quality of her speech pattern, her military bearing, and the very quiet calm of her recitation filled me with dread.

"What I'm going to tell you is not for the newspaper," she said, addressing Ted directly. "Is that clearly understood?"

Ted nodded his agreement, no more able to articulate his feelings than I was.

"It's not easy for me to talk about this. There were days I could not get out of bed, nights when I cried myself to sleep, then woke from dreams that scared me, dreams of running, of trying to get away, but never succeeding. The world seemed to be tumbling down on me, and I would sit alone and scream at the sky, and ask why. Why me?"

She paused here, as if gathering her thoughts, or, at least, the thoughts she wanted to share with us. She seemed, then, to straighten her shoulders, to lift herself a little higher from her already near-perfect posture. She looked from Ted to me, before taking a deep breath and continuing quietly. "I simply could no longer live that way, so I asked for help. And I found it, here. I've been seeing a Navy counselor. She has been a pillar for me, an avenue that led me to discover my real strength as a human being. She urged me to talk about what happened, not to keep it locked away, as if I had done something to hide. She convinced me that I would never be a whole person, never find my own power, never be my own true self, unless I found a way to get out from under what felt like a boulder crushing me. It has taken me a very long time to do what she has been urging me to do for a very long time, but in talking with her, I felt the burden become lighter, and so I knew she was right. That is the only reason I am speaking to you now."

She paused, again, before coming to the very edge of what she had to tell us. "Yes, talking about it helped me very much, but not enough by itself to lift that burden completely. I needed to confront him. And that is what I did."

The walls of her office seemed to get closer, closing in. I held my breath.

"Mr. Jeppards fathered me," she said. "Do you understand what I am telling you?"

"Your father!" It was like I was falling through an opening in the floor, down, down, down into a new reality. I wanted desperately to undo it, just as I had wanted to undo the memory of Soul Man's last act – a haunting exit, which I now understood, but wished I didn't.

"That designation carries a certain dignity, a sense of responsibilities discharged," she said, "so, no, he was in no way a father to me. I was barely more than a baby. I told him I was about to go public, and the coward could not handle it."

"Your mother?" I asked, though my voice seemed to come from somewhere else.

"No mother," she said. "Just him. My mother died when I was born."

Was this a test from that god I didn't believe in? First Ted, now Captain Arlington? I sat in stunned silence as I tried to rearrange the pieces of the puzzle that I had so carefully assembled. Soul Man had been with me, night and day, and now this ramrod straight Navy officer in full Parade Dress was describing... Whom? Certainly not the Soul Man of my quest. I could not quite comprehend what was happening before my eyes, before my ears.

"You asked if I knew him. Yes, I knew him," she continued. "I knew him the way the Bible uses that word. Or, rather, he knew me that way. I have kept this secret for too many years," she said, "as if I had done something to be ashamed of. I was a child. I should not have been introduced to shame so early."

Ted and I sat in stunned silence as she began to recite a litany of memories that sounded almost as if she had memorized them – or repeated so often in her mind that it had the quality of rote. There was almost no overt emotion as she spoke. Though the revelations came forth like bursts of water from a hand-pumped well, she remained dry eyed, her emotions tightly controlled.

"I was four years old," she said, "and he did things to me he called love." There was silence for a moment before she repeated, "Love."

And then those dark orbs that were her eyes stared straight into mine, penetrating my soul as Soul Man's eyes had done. I expected the same accusing hatred I had perceived in his eyes, but instead, I found myself looking into the eyes of a child trying to comprehend the incomprehensible. "What he called love started before I can even remember," she said, finally standing, our cue to leave. "I was five when they took him away and gave me to my great aunt. It was the best thing that ever happened to me."

I could feel my heart pounding in the silence that followed. As Ted and I stood to leave, the revulsion I felt for what JJ had done nauseated me. I thought I might throw up. How, I wondered, had this brave woman managed to come so far harboring her secret – his secret – in silence for so long?

Thoughts careened around my head like weighty pinballs. What is life and what is death? Such fluid terms, so imprecise. Where does a circle begin or end? Why had I done it, given up everything I knew and was comfortable with to pursue... what?

Again, I heard my own voice as if coming from some distant place. "What did you tell him?" I wanted to know, and immediately felt guilty for asking.

She pursed her lips. "It wasn't the first time I phoned him, you know. I had tried once before to confront him on the phone. He hung up on me that first time, slammed the phone down as if what I had to say was an annoyance he did not want to confront."

I flashed back to the strange conversation I had had at the VFW potluck. That young man, Rick I think his name was, had told me that Mr. Jeppards had been both distracted and disturbed. *Had he just hung up on his daughter,* I wondered. It was a fleeting thought, cut short when Captain Arlington continued.

"He could not acknowledge what he had done. He could not face it. He could not face himself."

"So what made you try again," I couldn't help interrupting.

There was a long pause before she seemed to make a conscious decision to unburden herself to us, as if at that moment she chose to see us as something more than mere strangers. "Between that first call and this one, I had taken another step I wanted to tell him about, a step he had a right to know about." She paused once again, before pushing the narrative to its conclusion. "I told him that I had informed his brothers about what he had done."

"His brothers? I thought..."

She interrupted my unfinished thought. "No, Sir," she said, reverting to military parlance, "not real blood brothers, but those whom I have discovered in my own career are much more valued. I am speaking about the brothers he served with, the brothers who bravely..." And here she interrupted her own thought to add, "Yes, I acknowledge their bravery, even Mr. Jeppards'. No man, nor any woman, is all one thing or another, all good or all bad. I find nothing to fault with these brothers who bravely refused illegal orders and went to prison for their refusal." She took a very deep breath before going on. "I found three still living members, three survivors of that close-knit group of men, that group of brothers. I found them and, one by one, I contacted them and, one by one, I let them know. And that is what I told Mr. Jeppards on the phone. I pulled the trigger," she concluded, "and I'm not sure what I feel at this moment about it all."

Time seemed to stand still. The three of us were each caught in his or her own thoughts, overwhelming thoughts. I felt as if I had split into two people, revolted by Mr. Jeppards, but clinging to the illusion I had created. Soul Man had been as real to me as Robinson Crusoe had been when I first read the book. I thought of him as a real person, someone who managed to survive on that island. When I learned later that he was a product of Defoe's imagination, I still could not stop thinking of him as a living person. I loved my creation. My Soul Man could never have done what Mr. Jeppards had done to Pearley, I like to think.

I had crossed JJ's path at the moment he decided he could bear no more, and because of that – and only because of that – do I have this story to tell. I saw his accusing eyes, and reflexively locked my car doors in fear. For my part of the story, it began there. But for him, the story began so much earlier – perhaps centuries earlier! Soul Proprietor had left an unbearable legacy that I had known nothing about, but even in his most vulnerable moment, he was still able to express his smoldering rage at me, symbol of a world that placed no value on him as a human being, and locked its doors against him.

And now I focused on that legacy, the Navy officer who stood on the other side of her desk, Captain Pearley Phyicia Arlington, and suddenly my mind closed the circle. "You're P.P."

The Captain slumped back into her chair. For the first time, tears began to pour down her face. "It's... it's what he called me," she gasped, trying but failing to regain her composure. And then, I, too, began to cry. There was so much to cry about. I had gone down a rabbit hole chasing a figment, a figment ennobled by each new detail that unfolded – until the very last detail. I had unearthed first a victim who, like all victims, both deserved and earned my sympathy. But in the end – in the beginning – my victim was the worst kind of victimizer. Not just against an innocent child, but his own innocent child! I can barely bring myself to write the words: the figment I had named Soul Man had molested his baby daughter!

Ted and I continued to stand there, he lost in his own dark memories, and me trying to put the world back together. I had got it all wrong, and in getting it all wrong, I had to experience JJ's death all over again. I had seen the flesh-and-blood man alive in front of me, then gone forever. But it wasn't forever because he had just died again.

Sitting at her desk was P.P. alternately losing then regaining control. She was pained, yes, but she had also prevailed, the two "Ps" that came to my mind. The child that Soul Man had called P.P. had killed him for all time, just as the cold, unforgiving waters of San Francisco Bay had killed the man she could not acknowledge as "father."

Her tears? Maybe for the memories of her brutal betrayal, or maybe the realization that her act of honesty, her courage to come clean, had led to that moment on the Bridge. I felt an overwhelming sense of sympathy for her, but also for myself. The man I invented, the man I wanted him to be, the man who righteously described himself as "Soul Proprietor" and I called Soul Man, that man was dead.

Ted cleared his throat, both because he had to and because we needed to leave Captain Arlington the little time she had left before the Parade. "I am truly sorry, Captain," he said, his voice breaking. "It never goes away, I can tell you from personal experience. But talking about it makes it easier."

"Yes," she agreed, "it does. I am sorry, too," she added, as we exited the office, leaving her alone with her thoughts.

# Epilogue

How strange life is. More than strange – depressing at times, confounding and painful, but at other times exhilarating, fantastic. What an amazing mystery it all is.

I'm sitting here at a small table under the stars in Lihui, the capital of Kauai, Hawaii's northern-most island, where my sometimes sweet and always generous sister has taken us. We are here – Kiki, Ted, Renni and I – to celebrate New Year's Eve, the turn of the century, the turn of the millennium. Renni and Kiki are dancing the macarena, gyrating among dozens of other couples. The evening is warm, and Ted and I are sipping cold Asahi beer imported from Japan, talking about my future as his assistant at the paper.

That's right; he's offered me a job working with him, and I've accepted the offer, though I know nothing about what it means to be a journalist. When I pointed this out to Ted, he smiled and said, "That's what makes good journalism. Knowing nothing means that you have to learn something, immerse yourself in a story, plumb its depths, then write what you've learned." I tried to protest, but he wouldn't have it. "You're going to be great at this," he said. I can't say that I share his prognosis, but his faith in me means much more than I would have thought.

On Christmas Day I called Perry and explained all that had happened. When I got to the part about Soul Man molesting Pearley, all he could manage was, "No, no, no... Not a brother!" All I could manage in return was, "Yes, yes, yes... A brother, a father, an uncle, a cousin."

He wasn't happy about my decision to take a new job in Honolulu. "So, you're abandoning the girls to swim with dolphins," he said, adopting an accusatorial tone. "Can I send you the ugly dog you foisted on us?"

"Not unless Lilla and the girls come with him."

"Be careful what you offer," he said, back in character. "We'll all show up on your doorstep one of these days." I took it as a promise.

"Aloha," I said. "Fuck you," he replied, before handing the phone to Lilla.

My call to Audrey at F.A.C.T. was briefer, but no less bittersweet.

"Harry," she gushed, "they want you back."

"Who wants me back?"

"They do. Everybody. Dorothy and the entire Board. Even Ms. Cabrillo wants you."

"What's the change of heart about?"

"On the morning of the Big Dinner, the *Chronicle* reprinted an article about you from the Honolulu paper. We sold every single table for the first time ever. And between then and now, donations just keep pouring in."

*Poetic injustice,* I thought, with some satisfaction. "Do me a favor, Sweetheart," I said. "Kiss Dorothy on all four cheeks for me, and tell her I wish her luck."

Who knows what tomorrow might bring? But here, now, sitting at this little table at the edge of the dance floor with my friend, watching my sister and her boyfriend swaying in tandem with the other dancers under the swaying palms, and breathing in the island's perfumed air, all I can think of is summed up in a single word:

Damn!

# THE END

# Acknowledgments

The idea to write *Soul of the Matter* is the direct result of my learning of the terrible carnage at Port Chicago, California, that occurred during WWII – a preventable munitions explosion that instantly incinerated 320 men. So, first, I want to acknowledge their unnecessary human sacrifice. More particularly, I am indebted to the 50 Black sailors who, afterwards, refused unlawful orders to resume loading their lethal cargo, risking – and receiving – long prison sentences in a Federal Penitentiary. One of the main characters in *Soul of the Matter* is a fictionalized member of this courageous group of men. It is their courage that gave me the courage to step out of my journalistic comfort zone to write this novel.

In writing the novel, I relied on so many others to help guide me through the process. In particular, the members of the Memoir Writing Group I have been a part of for a decade provided critical feedback all along the way. Although we are a collection of memoir writers – seniors, all – our members very graciously indulged my request to share each chapter of the novel with them. Following the reading of those chapters, they provided invaluable feedback, correcting misspellings, grammatical gaffes and typos, and asking probing questions that needed to be answered. Besides tightening the story and helping to bring the characters to life, they also unfailingly provided the encourage-ment that kept me moving forward. I owe all of them my gratitude.

While I am grateful for the support of everyone in that group, I am particularly indebted to Diane Reed, who not only participated in that ongoing process, but also took on the extra roles of editor, publicist, tech advisor and more. Unfailingly there for me, she provided both editorial and personal support throughout, praising my words when she thought praise was deserved, and challenging me when my words fell short. More than indebted, I am honored by her friendship.

I also want to acknowledge South Africa's Brenda Van Niekerk (Triomarketers) for the beautiful job she did designing the cover and laying out the text, as well as Jeremy Goody, at Megasonic Sound in Oakland, for engineering the high-quality audio recording I made of *Soul of the Matter*.

Of course, there are many other individuals who gave of themselves, reading the manuscript or listening to the audiobook, and then giving me their critical feedback. The danger in naming these people – especially for someone in his late 70s, a time when memory begins to fail – is that I will overlook one or another who should be listed here. To them, I apologize in advance. With that caveat, here are some of the people I want to acknowledge and thank for their contributions: Jan Bourret, Galen Ellis, Ali Moss and Patricia Nelson all listened to the audiobook of *Soul of the Matter* and responded with important suggestions that improved the book in so many ways. Similarly, Joe Sternfeld and *SF Chronicle* columnist and author, Kevin Fisher-Paulson, agreed to read the book and provide their honest assessments.

Finally, writing anything requires the forbearance and patience of family, especially when the process takes years to complete. Thank you, JC, my partner for over 40 years, for putting up with me

# About the Author

Michael A. Kroll is an award-winning journalist and story teller, specializing in issues of justice and injustice. Selected for "Special Recognition" by the Eugene Block Journalism Awards for "outstanding coverage of human rights issues," Kroll draws on those issues in *Soul of the Matter*, his first novel.

Having grown up in the beautiful Ojai Valley in Southern California, Kroll attended the University of California at Berkeley, majoring in political science and graduating in 1965, a few months after being arrested in the Free Speech Movement. He taught in an all-Chinese secondary school in the jungles of Malaysian Borneo for the Peace Corps, and taught Adult Education in East Los Angeles, Honolulu, New Orleans, Atlanta and Washington, D.C. Michael Kroll has fought against the death penalty and for criminal justice reform by working as a Mitigation Specialist in many death penalty cases, and heading such organizations as the National Moratorium on Prison Construction and the Death Penalty Information Center.

Michael Kroll has been published widely in newspapers from *The New York Times* to the *Los Angeles Times*, and in publications as disparate as *The Nation* and *Progressive* magazines on one hand, and *Women's World* on the other. Most recently, he has had memoir pieces published, including "McCarthyism Goes Postal," (*Ojai Quarterly*, winter 2015-'16) and "Land Snakes Alive," (*Trajectory Journal*, Spring 2018). He has a published book-length memoir, *Beijing and Beyond,* chronicling a 1981 tour of China's coming-of-age criminal justice system. These pieces, among others, can be found on his web page: www.michael-a-kroll.com[1].

Kroll leads writing workshops in juvenile halls, facilitates a memoir-writing group of seniors, and posts many of his published pieces on his website. In addition to writing, he also records as a Voice

---

1.     http://www.michael-a-kroll.com

Over artist from his home studio in Oakland, California. (michaelsvoice.net[2]).